First Edition, July 2023

10 9 8 7 6 5 4 3 2 1

FAC-004510-23152

Printed in the United States of America

This book is set in Garamond 3, Teebrush Paint, and Dinkle
Designed by Catalina Castro and Kurt Hartman

Library of Congress Control Number: 2022951029
ISBN 978-1-368-07435-3
Reinforced binding

Visit www.DisneyBooks.com
and Marvel.com

SUSTAINABLE FORESTRY INITIATIVE

Certified Sourcing

www.forests.org
SFI-01681

Logo Applies to Text Stock Only

Colin—For every Loki with a hidden hideout,
where the best secret stuff gets hid

Jackson—For Megan, who kept impossible hopes alive

Billy—For Rachel and Ellie,
my merry band of adventurers

CHAPTER 1

As recounted by Fandral, Bard of Bards

When I dream, I'm the hero.

I slay mighty giants in the icy fields of Jotunheim. I brave the blazes of Muspelheim and laugh in the face of Hel.

Between the hours of Nott and Morginn, the All-Father himself knows my name. We hang out. He thinks I'm awesome.

But every other time, from morning to night? Every other time . . .

1

. . . I'm just **Fandral**.

So, let's start with the big questions like: What's a Fandral? And more importantly, what's with that big beastie he's chasing? Well, that's a Chimera, and we'll get to it, but the answers to both of those questions start with a place.

Far beyond the realms of Midgard—that's where mere mortal humans live their oh-so-normal lives—there is a mega-giant-super-fantastically huge tree. Whole *worlds* grow off its branches like delicious fruit, with mountains and oceans and sometimes elves or Dwarves or humans! People in the know call it the World Tree. And if one has heard about the World Tree, then one has probably heard of the place that sits at the very top, gleaming with glory and made of living myth . . .

ASGARD.

As someone who grew up here, there are three rules in Asgard that I'll explain before our story gets properly started.

RULE 1: ODIN RULES

They don't call him the All-Father for nothing. The whole realm of Asgard is protected and ruled by Odin All-Father, King of the Aesir. He's not the actual dad of everyone in Asgard, even though he definitely acts like it. Just do what he says and try not to look him in the (one) eye.

RULE 2: WE'RE ALL GODS—
EXCEPT NOT REALLY

Confused? Don't worry. Being confused about Asgard is a time-honored human tradition! People have been worshipping us since the Vikings, but the truth is that we're more like very powerful, extremely long-lived people. We're all stronger than humans, we live a lot longer, we look better in gold—we're gods with a lowercase g. The only Capital-G Gods are those who prove themselves worthy to live in the Palace of Odin, where they get cool powers and go on wild adventures and generally live lives filled with awesome. The rest of us are, at least by Asgardian standards, pretty normal.

So what's a Fandral? He's me. A normal kid from Asgard, son of a warrior in the great army of Odin. He lives in Lower Asgard, he grew up in the shadow of a golden palace filled with Gods, and he isn't a big fan of the taste of goat. And he is currently breaking Rule #3 of Asgard.

RULE 3: MONSTERS DON'T BELONG IN ASGARD

For all eternity, since Asgard was first settled at the top of the World Tree, it's been official policy that monsters are 100 percent off-limits. No dragons, no serpents, no dragon-headed serpents or serpent-headed dragons no matter how cool they look or what gold they promise you. Of course, there's one exception to this rule: my uncle Leif.

See, my uncle Leif has a weird job: He's the Master of the Great Asgardian Menagerie ("menagerie" is fancy schmancy for "zoo").

People from all over the realms come to see the weird and wonderful creatures collected by the valiant hunters of Ullr. He's forgetful and has a whole ton of problems to deal with every day, so about once a week . . . something escapes from Uncle Leif's zoo.

And then I have to catch it.

The problem right now? This isn't some escaped flying badger (that was last week); this is a freakin' Chimera! Chimeras are the worst parts of a dragon and a duck and a dog all splurched together. They have feathers, but they can't fly. They have teeth, but they're inside a beak.

7

Leif calls him Jeff.
I hate Jeff.

I leap across the rooftops, grabbing at the leash—but Jeff's giant duck feet are *shockingly fast*. I'm maybe the sixth-fastest kid in Lower Asgard and I'm barely keeping up! Jeff the Speedy Chimera might have a future in professional racing, but I won't be alive to see it after my parents find out their favorite longhouse is now a stylish pile of bricks.

The horns of the City Watch blare in the distance. Jeff lets out his version of a roar—it's really more of a super-terrifying *quack*—and perches on top of an old armory. The metal roof will hold him, but the minute he jumps down into the street, it's gonna be chaos. And there's no way—*no way*—the Watch is gonna get here in time.

Leaping off the rooftop, I reach one last time for the leash . . . but I'm too slow! Jeff is already leaping down to the street below, and me after him!

I take a huge breath. I'm gonna be in *so much trouble*.

And then I hear the thunder.

RUMBLE! RUMBLE! RUMBLE!

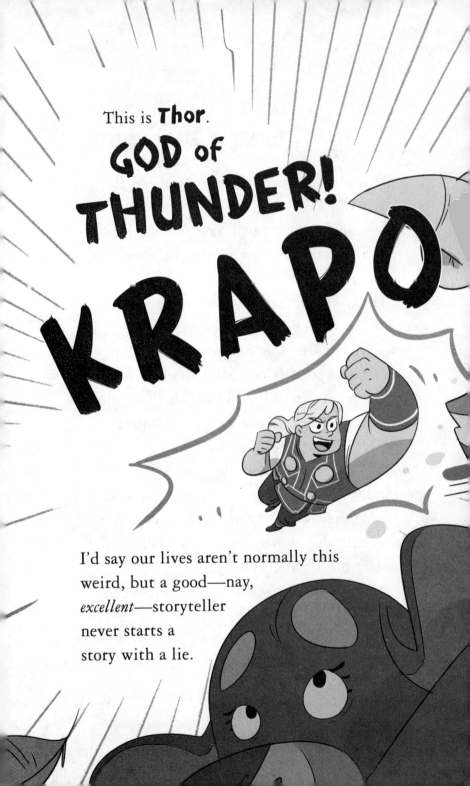

This is **Thor**.

GOD of THUNDER!

KRAPO

I'd say our lives aren't normally this weird, but a good—nay, *excellent*—storyteller never starts a story with a lie.

Thor makes it look easy. He grabs the big duck feet and flips the beast upside down, pinning it swiftly with a thunderclap.

And then Thor poses.

HOW DO YOU LIKE THAT?!

Not his best, but it'll do.

Thor is the most awesome, impressive, popular, did-I-mention-*awesome*? kid in the Nine Realms. Every kid in Asgard wants to be him, fight beside him, or get a glimpse of him in action. It's not just because he's got the natural charisma of a guy who can take down a Chimera, but because he's the Real-Life Prince of Asgard. Remember how I said Odin wasn't our actual dad? Well, that's true for everyone *except* Thor.

And technically Loki. But more on that later.

Someday, hundreds of years from now probably, Thor will be the All-Father. He'll talk all fancy and sit on a throne and, everywhere he goes, there'll be fanfares and banners and a hundred attendants. But right now?

He's just my best friend.

"Did you see that, Fandral?! That dragon-creature fought like a *duck*!"

I decide not to tell him it was actually mostly a duck-creature. Why hurt his feelings?

"We should get this back to your uncle's zoo, right? Before my father's guards get here and ruin everything?" Thor steps off Jeff's chest, and the Chimera stirs a bit. Jeff's dazed, but not for long.

Unfortunately, we're not going anywhere. Because while *kids* think Thor is supercool,

the adults whose houses just got smashed courtesy of Thor Odinson don't seem to agree.

They surround us on both sides. Judging by their expressions, we're gonna be stuck on Sigrid Street cleanup duty for the next eighty-five years. Obviously not an ideal outcome, but not every problem can be solved with a thunder-powered punch.

That's where I come in.

See, I may not be the fastest or the strongest or the smartest kid in Asgard, but I do something even more important: I *listen*.

I hear the skalds when they tell the old tales, and I memorize my favorite lines. I've learned the runes and drawn the sigils, and I'm not too bad with calligraphy. I know all the old legends and am pretty good at telling them in front of a roaring fire to the delight of young and old. I'm what some cultures call a bard, a storyteller, a Keeper of History's Mysteries.

Not sure how that's supposed to save the day? Let me demonstrate.

Heyyyyyyy, folks!

I know you're mad. I'd be mad too, but I think we can all agree that the alternative would've been much worse. My uncle Leif sends his most sincere apolog—

BOOOOOOOOOOO!!!

I don't think they're buying it, buddy.

Okay, plan B.

The Mighty Thor has saved you from a beast of immeasurable power! And to help you understand why you mustn't let him be punished for the aftermath...

...I'll tell you a story.

WHAAAAAAAAAAAAAAAAA

When I was just a wee babe, I escaped my home!

In the streets of Asgard, I was lost and confused! But I've always had a voice fit for boasting, so I used my tiny lungs to call out for help!

My terrified wailing was so powerful that it shook storefronts and rattled rafters! And the All-Father had no chance of arriving before I destroyed the whole neighborhood with my cry!

But luckily, Thor was there.

He comforted me! Told me that I knew I was lonely, but that I didn't need to bring down the All-Father's help. After all...

You have a friend with you already.

And from that day forth, your prince has been an honorable protector of this city! Powerful, of course. Wise? Sure!

But above all else, Thor is kind. He is a good friend.

So, What do you say?

If you won't cheer your prince, will you at least support and cheer on your friend?

What can I say?
I have a way with
people.

We throw a rope on the Chimera and start guiding it through the backstreets. It's hard to move a big beast like that without causing the poor creature any more discomfort than we already have by catching it, but with a little teamwork, Thor and I can do just about anything. We try to be extra careful not to attract any more attention, which is pretty tough when you're leading around a giant monster, but I've spent my entire life in Lower Asgard, so I know the best ways to get around.

"That was close. My dad can't find out about this or I'll lose city privileges for sure," says Thor.

"He won't find out," I say. "The story'll keep everyone quiet about what really happened."

"Wild how much people want to be my friend, right? What dorks," Thor says as we step into an alley to rest.

And then he smiles, ear to ear. The troublemaking kid I know comes out, replacing the posing warrior prince he puts on for the rest of the world.

"Seventeen minutes, cage to capture," says Thor. "That's a new record."

"You know the point is to give the creature exercise, right?" But I see it in Thor's eyes. It's a challenge that lies in the heart of a hero—the same one I see in the beasts from my uncle's menagerie when they get to pit themselves against the might of the young god. Against that noble look, I can't help but give in. "Fine, fine. Seventeen minutes. You think you can beat it tomorrow?"

"Always. After all, didn't you hear that awesome story? I'm the Mighty Thor."

We lead Jeff the Chimera back into my uncle's fancy petting zoo for strange creatures (and the occasional monster).

"You know, I've been thinking we ought to give one of the other monsters a shot at the title. Next time," says Thor, "let's release the *dragon*."

CHAPTER 2

A tale told by Sif, Warrior of the Vanir

"Sif of the Vanir," intones the voice of my mother. "Are you ready to take your first steps into legend?"

"Yes," I say, knowing it to be true.

Everyone I have ever known is assembled outside our home. They fill the large path that stretches into the woods beyond, the whole of the Vanir. They are my mothers, my sisters, my brothers, my elders. They are the Old Gods, nestled in their corner of the World Tree. Vanaheim, forgotten but never broken. My mother moves to stand among them. To lead them on their procession to the Farewell Stone.

But they do not move, the Vanir. Not yet.

They are waiting for me.

I feel the fear. A sudden surge of unworthiness: I'm not enough; I'll never be enough for what my people need of me. I'm not up to this. I've fought my entire life for this day—for this honor—and now that it's here, I do not know how I can live up to my own expectations, let alone those of my ancestors. My breath quickens. The fear comes from my heart and heads for my mind. Along the way, I feel it catch in my chest.

Unbidden, like instinct, my fourth mother's voice comes into my mind.

If you can feel it, you can control it.

If you can control it, you can master it.

If you can master it, you can use it with honor.

I close my eyes. I slow my breathing. I try
to will my heart to beat less. And while I still
have much to learn, I know enough. The fear
is contained.

I open my eyes, and my people are
still there. Still watching. But I don't see
judgment anymore.

I see pride.

And I feel hope.

We do not have the glory of Asgard, but
we have the spirit of Vanaheim. And that's
more than enough.

My first mother leads the story I've heard once before: three years ago, when my brother bid his Farewell.

"Before the Aesir rose through war and toil of men to the top of the World Tree, to sit on their thrones in Asgard, it was we, the Vanir, who kept nature in balance."

And the whole procession sings, *"We keep the tree."*

"The Nine Realms only thrive now because we tended them for eternities beforehand. Though Odin is All-Father, we are every mother."

"We keep the tree."

"And so though we work in obscurity, though they call us the Old Gods, the golden palace of Asgard is mastered not just by their king, Odin, but by our queen, Freya! Goddess of Life! Goddess of War!"

"She keeps the tree."

When I say those last words, I can't help but smile. I'm going to meet her. Freya's going to know my name.

Awesome.

THE FAREWELL STONE

The procession ends in a small clearing, dominated by the Farewell Stone. This place has been held sacred by my people ever since Odin and Freya's marriage, when it was placed here as a link between our peoples. It's a reminder that we are all gods, and that our queen's home and hearth are always open to the Vanir.

I remember Heimdall's bravery as he stepped into the stone. He looked grown-up, ready to take on entire worlds if he was called upon. I vow to be so valiant that I make *him* look like a coward.

And I vow to tease him about it when I see him on the other side.

"Come forth, Sif," says my first mother,

beckoning me to the glowing circle of magic cast by the Farewell Stone. I've never been so near to it. They say you can feel the golden glow of Asgard. I'm delighted to find that they're right.

"Each year, one of our young Outriders proves themself worthy to walk the halls of Freya's Keep and learn at her hand. The trials have been completed, the games are over, and one champion stands among the youth of Vanaheim. Master of sword and shield. Rider of great beasts. Lover of sweet snacks."

My mother beams proudly as a ripple of quiet laughter travels through the crowd. "My daughter," she says. "Sif."

There is no applause at my name. Only a reverent hush that falls over everyone assembled. This whole day is sacred to us, but this next moment . . . this is the important stuff. I've been identified as the Ascended, she who sits at the feet of Freya, welcomed into the halls of the Gods.

My sisters in the Freyan Outriders, the girls I beat out for this honor, are watching with a mix of pride and jealousy. After all, I'll spend the entire summer in Asgard learning from the best.

But I will not venture alone. All those who ascend are given a vinr, a gift that acts as a traveling companion of sorts.

These gifts are legendary. They're the greatest honor that can be bestowed on a Vanir of my age. Growing up, I learned all about the most distinguished among them. . . .

OAKEN WARSHIP OF THE EVERSEA

A boat! A whole, actual boat! Gifted to the first ascended Vanir, Njord, the Oaken Warship was said to be capable of fitting in Njord's pocket when he wished—but when it was thrown into any sea, it would become the strongest, largest longship Asgard had ever seen. It helped Njord become the God of the Sea in Odin's pantheon. I had a model above my crib growing up. I used to pretend that if I threw it into the sea, I could sail to Asgard myself.

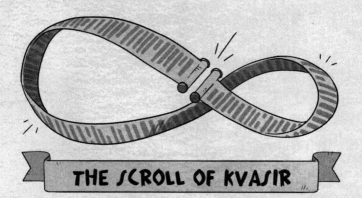

THE SCROLL OF KVASIR

I'm not one for poems and stories, but if I were, the Scroll of Kvasir would be a dream given form. A book that never ends, filled with every story and poem in the entire World Tree. They said its bearer went on to become the God of Poetry, though the stories of how he achieved it were different every time.

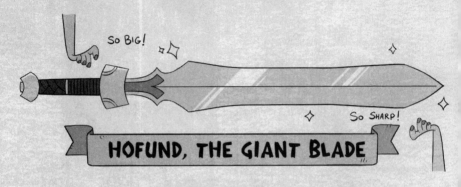

So Big!

So Sharp!

HOFUND, THE GIANT BLADE

My brother got a giant sword. He named it Hofund. And when I say it was giant, I mean it was literally built to be used by a giant. It was honestly a little goofy-looking; he could barely hold it. To him, it was a greatsword. To a giant, it was probably a toothpick. But I gotta be honest, I was still very jealous of it.

I resolved years ago that though Heimdall was the first through to Freya's service, I would be the first in our family to earn a place of responsibility among the Gods—and now my time is coming. My second mother, the priest of our clan, removes a box from her cart and brings it to me. Every step sends a spike of excitement down my spine.

I've thought for years about what might await me as my vinr.

A huge ax capable of cutting the head off a Muspel Fire Troll?

Boots that could outrun time?

My very own suit of plate armor?

But when I open the box . . .

. . . it's better than I could've ever hoped.

"His name is **Wygul.** He will grow large enough to ride, and wise enough to understand your every word. But first—"

"I must train him," I cut in. I can't help myself. "As Freya trained her great cat-beasts Bygul and Trjegul before they could pull her chariot into battle."

"Just so," says my second mother, with pride.

Wygul puts a single paw on my forehead. A greeting—and maybe, with the press of his claws, a warning not to get too familiar too fast.

"He's fierce. Like me." I grin. "I love him. Thank you, Mother."

She bows her head.

"I love you, Sif. We all do. And remember, we will continue to love you, no matter what."

That *fear* again. But I cage it. I do not break my mother's glance.

"I won't let you down."

My second and first mothers step back, beyond the circle. The bestowing is done.

I turn to the assembled crowd. I bow. I swear to them that I'll make them proud. And finally, I look up, channeling my fear into excitement and wielding it with honor.

...you are in Asgard.

It's **Heimdall**!
I knew I would see
him again, but I never
guessed it would be
so soon. My instinct is
to run to him—I just
want to hug my big
dumb brother and tell
him how much I missed
him, like *so much*—but
then I see it.

He's operating the Bifrost. My brother,
Heimdall, the Heimdall who used to
put lizards in my shoes and call them
"scaleyshoes," *that* Heimdall . . . is now the
Guardian of the Bifrost. He's not smiling, no
big inviting warm arm out to his sister. He's
on duty. He's *working*.

I keep it together. This is big. I don't want
to embarrass him or myself.

I walk up to him.

Bow.

And in my most official voice, I say the words I know everyone's waiting to hear.

"Guardian of Asgard, All-Seeing Eye of the Bifrost, I, Sif of the Vanir, seek passage to Asgard."

My brother doesn't smile. I hope he's just putting on an act. Could Asgard have possibly changed him so much?

"I saw you coming, Sif of the Vanir. As I saw your companion, Wygul. As I now see all things in the World Tree."

He has changed. His voice is soft, calming, friendly. But he's so severe.

"And you are both most welcome here. The All-Mother awaits . . . in the Palace."

He bows. Waves his arm to the city, as if telling me to explore. And he smiles. Just a little. It's enough. I can see him in there. Which means if I'm going to beat him to Odin's pantheon . . .

I'm going to have to work even harder than I thought.

My first day in Asgard is
awesome. Obviously.
But nothing can possibly live
up to the end of the day.

THE
FIGHTING PITS
THE. LITERAL BEST.
PLACE!

THE ROW OF
MEADS AND
HONEY

Lots of grown-ups. Not a lot of fun.
Wygul chased a rat.

LOWER ASGARD

THE
INFINITE SEA

BIFROST
Heimdall works here.
No fun, just grumpy.

When I finally reach the palace, Heimdall is right: They're expecting me. The guards of Asgard, in their giant golden helmets (with way too many antlers), move their big spears out of the way and let me pass into the golden hall of Odin.

It's breathtaking. Walls of gold. Floors of glass. All of it humming with power.

This is where the Gods live.

This is where I *belong*.

And at the end of the chamber, a mighty throne. Not the golden one the mortals of Midgard revere, adorned with two ravens and sat upon by the King of Asgard, but a beautiful wooden seat carved from the very wood of the World Tree. At one side sits a black cat the size of an elephant. On the other, his twin. Bygul and Trjegul.

Wygul bows his head to them.

I bow mine to the occupant of the throne itself.

Freya.

She knows my name she knows my name she knows my name holy cats she knows my *NAME*.

"Queen Freya. It's an honor."

Her smile is so kind it warms Wygul's fur.

"The honor is mine, child. They say you are the greatest young warrior my Outriders have ever produced. Our Vanir hopes for a hero, fulfilled. I have long awaited your journey into the halls of Asgard . . ."

I feel like my heart is going to burst

". . . but I'm afraid I have some bad news."

And then it does.

"Um . . . Bad news, my queen?"

Her face changes.

I know that look. It's the look an adult gets right before they tell you something they know you don't want to hear. It's the we're-eating-liver-for-dinner look. It's the training's-canceled-today look. It's the we-got-your-brother-a-sword-and-not-you look.

And now Freya is making it. To me.

"I'm afraid I cannot take you into my direct training and service."

My heart sinks.

"The realms are in a state of chaos beyond this place. Wars rage between the Light Elves of Alfheim and the Dark Elves of Svartalfheim, between the tribes of Midgard, between the Jotun and the Muspel. Betrayal even stains the Dwarf halls of Nidavellir. In all the realms, only our people and Asgard are not embroiled in battle. And it is my duty, my honor, and my privilege, to oversee these wars as the Goddess of Battle. I will not be in Asgard this summer. And I cannot take you into battle without risking your life, one that is far too precious to the Vanir and the Aesir alike. I am sorry."

Wygul looks at me, confused. I don't know how to answer. All I can see is the life I outlined for myself falling away, piece by piece, with every word out of Queen Freya's mouth. This summer, I was supposed to be Freya's apprentice! I was going to learn how to be a God—and become the youngest ever to sit in the pantheon of Odin! I earned this! And now I'm supposed to spend my summer doing what exactly?!

**OFFICIAL ASGARDIAN
CAT HERDER**

**FIGHTING PIT
WATERGIRL**

**ASSISTANT TO THE
KEEPER OF THE BIFROST**

**PALACE LIBRARY
GOPHER**
(NOT THE FUN ANIMAL KIND,
THE BORING JOB KIND)

SLEIPNIR STABLEGIRL

MAGICAL RAVENSITTER

GOLD JANITOR

FORGOTTEN STUDENT WHO WAS SUPPOSED TO BE IMPORTANT AND HAVE A SUPERCOOL SUMMER BUT NOW JUST HAS TO HANG OUT WITH NO PURPOSE AND DO NOTHING OF IMPORTANCE AT ALL.

brush brush

That fear I'd controlled back in Vanaheim? The one I'd mastered so I could use it honorably?

I can feel my hold over it slipping away. Tears are welling up in my eyes, but I bite the inside of my cheek, holding them back. A few more minutes and I'm going to embarrass myself, my brother, my family the whole of the Vanir. All because I can't deal with disappointment. Which makes *me* a disappointment, doesn't it?

Queen Freya stands. I hope she hasn't seen my tears, but I know she has. She's regarding me now. Thinking. For a moment, I wonder if I'm about to be cast out for dishonoring my people.

"But perhaps there is a different way you could learn from the Gods, mighty Sif."

I practically stop breathing.

"Anything, my queen."

Freya kneels next to me. She's so *tall*. And she smells of elderflower.

"You may have heard stories of my children. Baldr the brave, God of Light. Tyr the Strong,

God of War. Loki the Clever, God of Lies. But among them, none are as powerful—nor as reckless—as Thor."

That name was familiar. It was said when the sky roared in Vanaheim, that was young Thor crying in his crib.

"He is no longer a babe, yet he has not come into his power as a warrior. He is brave, but he is also foolhardy and impulsive. And the winds of fate tell me that soon he will be swept into adventures that he may not survive without keen eyes at his side. Without a sword that has proven itself. Without . . ."

"Me," I answer. "Without me."

Queen Freya smiles at me, and I try really hard not to melt.

"Your mission, given to you by the Queen of the Gods, is this: Watch over Thor Odinson for his absent mother. Raise your sword in defense of him, and keep him from making the kind of mistakes that would get him killed . . . or worse, endanger all of Asgard. Keep him safe . . . and more importantly, keep him honorable." Her eyes twinkle with sincerity. "Perhaps as he teaches you the ways of the Aesir . . . you might teach him a bit of the Old Ways. Hm?" She looks at me expectantly.

While I cannot help but feel like I just got handed a babysitting job to make up for losing my dream gig, I nod. "Yes, my queen. I shall."

I assume that's the end of it, that I'll be dismissed from here, free to return to the fighting pits and punch something for a while. But when Freya takes my hand, I realize the journey is just . . . beginning.

Now.

"Come, Sif," she says. "I'll take you to meet Thor."

CHAPTER 3

As recounted by Fandral, Bard of Bards

You know how sometimes you have a really great idea and then you do it, and everything turns out great?

This is like that . . . except for the part where it turns out great. Because that is *not* what's happening.

What's happening is Thor's dad. The big guy with the one eye. Odin himself.

And he is, let's say . . . not happy? Furious,

more like. And he's the King of the Gods, so when I say that he's so mad he's throwing lightning bolts? Trust me, I'm not being poetic; he is throwing *actual* lightning bolts.

It turns out that releasing a dangerous Chimera across town to test Thor's emergency-response time was maybe not the best idea.

Even though no one got hurt *and* Thor caught it *and* we even got it back into its pen before anyone noticed it was gone . . . well, we hoped word wouldn't get back.

Look, in hindsight, not our best move.

"What do you have to say for yourself?" rumbles Odin, his voice like thunder. I know he's talking to Thor, but if there's even a small chance I can protect my friend from his dad's fury, I have to take it.

"Lord Odin," I say before I can stop myself. "It was I who released the Chimera, not Thor—"

KRAKOOM.

My eyes take a moment to readjust from the flash of that lightning bolt, unleashed from Odin's great spear, Gungnir. It's said that the spear is the embodiment of lightning itself. I thought that was, you know, metaphorical—but clearly not. That was just about the biggest SHUSH of my life—and its meaning was 100 percent clear. *Odin doesn't want my input.*

Message received. Kind of rude, but I guess when you're the King of the Gods, you don't need to worry about a warrior's son. Even a warrior's son as cool as me. Or, if not cool, at least *dashing*.

"Thor!" rumbles Big Daddy Odin. "If this was the first time, perhaps we could claim it as a singular mistake. Twice . . . your mother and I thought, 'We can work with this.' But this is the *third time this month*! When will you learn that this kind of troublemaking, grandstanding behavior does not befit your station?"

Odin shakes his head, closing his eye in irritation. "You are a prince! You are my son! And you are grumble roar blah blah my name's Odin and I'm so loud and look at my lightning I'm so tough and . . ."

Whoops, sorry. I stopped paying attention to what the old man was talking about. The details aren't really important, because I get it, and Thor does too. But here's the point, the thing that Odin will never understand about his son: Thor doesn't really care about any of that title, station, royalty stuff. Being a prince means sitting around and following rules and playing it safe. Thor doesn't want to be a prince. He wants to be a *hero*. And if there's one thing the tales of Asgard tell us over and over again, it's this:

Apparently, heroes also don't keep their mouths shut. No one really needs to know what Thor and Odin start yelling at each other, but it's intense. And not just because of the actual electricity pinging around the room. Honestly, it's a little uncomfortable.

My gut says this isn't going to end well. Specifically, this isn't going to end well for me. Because when Thor gets grounded, he has to stay in a castle. When *I* get grounded, I have to spend the entire weekend picking up my brothers' dirty socks and making slop for the warpigs.

I'm in trouble. I know it. Thor knows it. And for some reason, he won't stop making it a bigger and bigger deal. I'm starting to put together a sock-cleaning schedule for the next month when, suddenly there's a cough at the door; Odin and Thor both fall silent mid-sentence. All three of us turn to find—

Queen Freya. And she isn't alone.

"Thor, I'd like you to meet someone," she says, stepping into the room. "She's of the Vanir, trained by my Outriders and here to receive education in the way of the Gods. This is Lady Sif. . . ."

You know that feeling when you're swinging a sword, but then your target moves at the last minute,

so your sword hits nothing and you're thrown completely off-balance? Where you know exactly what's going on one minute, and then the next you're spinning around and looking like a total dork?

Well, this is that feeling.

See, I'm all for meeting new people. And this girl seems pretty cool, actually. I mean, the Freyan Outriders are no joke. But in a single moment, with just a few words, Queen Freya changes *everything*. . . .

"Sif is to be your new companion."

Thor and I lock eyes.

BEST FRIEND PSYCHIC CONVERSATION!
(Except not really...
because neither of us is psychic)

"We're not saying that you and your friend Fandral can't spend your days together anymore. We're just saying perhaps you should think of different ways to spend that time in the company of more . . . responsible individuals." I can tell that Queen Freya is both highly attuned to our Best Friend Frequency and is also trying not to hurt my feelings. Which is actually really nice of her. Odin? Not so much a fan of the whole "Fandral's feelings" thing.

"You hear that, Thor?" Odin asks. "You need someone in your life who is a better influence." He looks over to me, his electric gaze still storming with displeasure. "I don't know if it's Fandral dragging you into trouble, or the other way around, but when you're together . . ."

KRAKOOM.

"Trouble!" Odin grumbles. He appraises the three of us carefully. "Here's how it's going to be," he says to Thor. "Sif is going to be your shadow. Where you go, she goes. And if you're not sure if something is a good idea or not . . . listen to her, *not* Fandral."

Ouch.

"Maybe you'll learn something. At the very least maybe you won't destroy any more market carts."

Odin is done with the conversation, I guess. He walks over to Freya and the two of them leave us alone.

With her.

When you're face-to-face with a wild animal, you're really not supposed to make eye contact. Because if you do, the animal thinks you're trying to start something. And as soon as you look away? Yeah, that wild animal is coming for you. Thor and I learned that the hard way—doesn't matter if a griffin is a baby, that bird-cat's got claws.

Anyway, this is like that. Except Thor and Sif are *both* animals. And whichever one flinches first . . . let's just say, it'll be *wild*.

. . . Okay, sorry, bad joke, I know. But I'm really nervous here, so cut me some slack.

Thor's the first to speak up. "I don't need a babysitter."

"Then why are you acting like a baby?" Sif retorts.

I step in, backing him up. "Hey!" I say, "That's Thor you're talking too! God of freaking thunder! He's not a baby. He's a big boy!"

Wait a minute. That doesn't sound right. I try again.

"He's a man! A big . . . boy . . . man!"

Look, I did *tell you* I was nervous.

Fandral... Dude.

Yeah, that got away from me, my bad.

Sif steps back, looking down her nose at both of us. She smells like wet forest and cat hair. It's around that time I notice the actual cat at her feet, looking at me like I might make a tasty snack. I know better than to mess around with Vanaheim cats. They're almost as scary as Vanaheim *girls*.

"Listen, you two," Sif says. "This isn't what I wanted either. I came here to train with your mother, the most impressive and dangerous woman in any of the Nine Realms. But she's so busy cleaning up your messes and overseeing conflict in the realms that she doesn't even have *time* to be awesome, let alone train *me* to be awesome. So instead, I get to chase you two around to keep you from . . . I don't know, juggling fire orbs or something."

Thor cuts his eyes to me and super quietly asks, "Fandral, can we get fire orbs?"

"You know we can, bud," I say as I make little explode-y hands.

AWESOME THINGS TO DO WITH FIRE ORBS

JUGGLING

BOWLING
(SUPER DANGEROUS)

MAKE EVEN BIGGER

ALL OF THE ABOVE, BABY!

"I saw that," says Sif, sounding a *lot* like Odin all of a sudden. "No. Fire. Orbs."

"Look, you're the one who had the idea," Thor says.

Sif turns red. Like, really red. It's clear to anyone in the vicinity, cat included, that she's mad and the sword on her hip isn't just for show.

"I can't *believe* you," she says. "I thought, 'Thor, Prince of Asgard, maybe he's actually, I don't know, worthy of the title?!' Instead, I find some . . . brat!"

Remember when I had all those really great lightning and electricity puns earlier? Yeah, the room feels like that again, but this time it's Thor, not his dad. The look in his eyes? *Shocking*.

"That's it. We're done here," Thor says, starting to walk away. "We're leaving. And, Lady *Sniff*? Don't even try to follow us." He glares at her. "This city is a maze. How embarrassing would it be to get lost *and* lose me on your first day?"

Sif's resolve wavers for a split second.

"Stay out of our way," says Thor, "and we'll stay out of yours, plus we'll tell my parents whatever they want to hear. I don't need a second friend. I got Fandral. And the two of us? We're all we need."

And then we storm out. I can't help but feel a little bad about the whole thing. After all, Sif's new, alone in a big city, without any friends or people to watch out for her.

But in my head, another voice pops up. One that sounds an awful lot like my best friend. *How is that our problem?* it says.

No one tells Thor what to do.

CHAPTER 4

A tale told by Sif, Warrior of the Vanir

"Oh yeah? I'm going to get lost? You can get lost . . . with my fist!"

I'd left the Throne Room as quickly as I'd been able and headed to the nearest training yard. No better way to hear myself think than to feel myself fight.

When I get frustrated, I know exactly which awesome martial arts move to do. I execute a perfect two-punch combination, knocking a big mushroom right off this massive tree.

"Stay out of the way . . . of my sword!"
Overhead strike! Cutting twist! Backflip! Yes!

I'm trying to adjust to the fallout of my
dreams for this summer colliding with the
God of Blunder. I mean, what right does a
spoiled, *know-nothing, trouble-making*—

In short, I'm upset about it. And where
I'm from, when you're upset, you grab your
sword and . . .

That ignorant prince was worse than the rudest stable hand I've ever met. In fact, I don't think I've ever met a stable hand that was anywhere *near* that rude! Actually, almost every stable hand I've ever met has been very well-mannered! Why am I talking about stable hands?!

Because I'm upset, and you need to accept my process.

I execute another two-strike combination, carving bark from the massive tree root I'm crawling over. I do a somersault flip right over the log, three-point landing. That's not something they teach you, by the way. Landing like that is *instinct*.

Warrior instinct.

I grip the hilt of my sword, held in my family since time immemorial and named by every new warrior who wields it. I call it Claw. Sharp as anything, and fast. The hilt is old, bronze, crafted to look like a lion's paw. Okay, technically a cat's paw, but my family have been members of the Outriders for centuries, so most of our stuff is kind of cat-themed.

"Mrow?!" As if I could possibly forget about him, Wygul yowls at me. So demanding.

"MROW?!?" A hiss escapes his bared kitty teeth, his tail becoming the kind of total floof that warns an Outrider of danger. We call it the warfloof.

I whip around, my sword swinging through the air, catching the sun,

LOKI.

Hello.

Did you mean for your sword to catch the sun like that?

I hope so, it looked totally awesome.

I've been warned about him. Well, not warned, but . . . informed. Strongly.

This is Thor's brother, Odin's youngest son. Back home, they call him a trickster, which is kind of a weird thing to call somebody when there is probably so much more going on with them than just the one thing? Then again, Thor is just one thing (a stubborn privileged blockhead), so maybe this one is just as bad.

"You already know me; I can tell." Loki's voice is smooth as silk—and just as slippery. "Saves me the hassle of introductions, which are a drag anyway, so thanks. In fact, I can speed it up even more: Your name is . . . the Lady Sif!!!"

It takes me only a moment to realize that he's not reading my mind or predicting the future. "Your mother told you."

He nods, skipping up to the top of a root, balancing on the edge. "My mother sent a pigeon that informed an ant that got word to me that, yes, your name was Sif and you would be spending the summer with the most boring family of Gods in Asgard."

Loki shoots me a look. "Spoiler alert: That's us."

After a moment, he starts moving deeper into the wood, stepping backward without hesitation. "I mean it, though. You handled that sword like a champ, sharp moves. But you were also taking some serious shots at an innocent tree . . . and in my experience, the only thing that can make someone that angry around here is my sweet brother. So . . . let me guess: You've already met Thor?"

I don't let my expression waver. Loki might be Thor's younger brother, but he is still a prince of Asgard. And I was raised with manners.

"My encounter with your brother was eventful, but pleasant. I . . . look forward to meeting him again."

"Ha!" Loki snorts, shaking his head. "Look, m'lady, there can only be one liar around here, and that's kind of my thing."

And then he turns into a cat.

"Truth is really wild, isn't it?"

Yes, the cat is talking to me. Talking cat. That is also a god.

This never happens back home.

"You think you know something, like who someone is," says cat-Loki, "and then they just prove to be someone else."

"You're a cat."

"I'm a cat *right now*. I feel like being a cat. Cat life is great. I mean, you're an Outrider, you get it. Sunbeams, chase bugs . . . Did I mention sunbeams?" Cat-Loki stretches the big stretch.

"A cat has zero responsibilities, sure," I say. "But you know what? No responsibilities, lazy, chases bugs . . . sounds like Thor, don't you think?"

He shudders. "Yeah, I don't think I'm supposed to be a cat."

Once again, Loki changes forms, turning back into a person, but different this time.

She is clearly waiting for me to say
something. I should say something. But what
am I supposed to say? I've seen magic, sure, but
. . . I never really considered that magic could
be used to change yourself into a different . . .
yourself. But I've got to say something, so I say
the first thing that comes to me:

"It *is* cool." Loki grins, and I get the feeling that isn't the standard reaction. "But not as cool as where I'm going to take you next. Come on, new girl."

I follow. "Can I ask," I start tentatively, "what do I call you in this form?"

"You mean pronouns?"

I nod.

Loki's thoughtful for a second. "Like this? She/her works. Like before? He/him's fine. They/them is always good."

"Got it." I nod again. "Cool."

She leads me deeper into the woods.

Woods?

Okay, wait. I know I had been in the city, but I guess I'd become so upset that I had gotten turned around. Ugh, gross—I guess Thor was kind of right; this place really is a maze. Loki's explaining it, pointing things out as we go, but then I stop dead in my tracks, taking in where we are: "Wait," I say. "Is this. . . ?"

"The World Tree?" Loki fills in. "Yeah, I was wondering when you'd notice that." She smiles as she leans against a mossy root.

"As in—?"

"As in the tree that unites all the realms?" Loki arches an eyebrow. "The very same."

I can't believe it.

I'd been chopping mushrooms off at the single most important tree in all of creation. The center point of the galaxy, which all Vanir are fated and charged to protect! And I was just using it for *TARGET PRACTICE*?!

Fear swells in my chest—if Loki tells *anyone*, I could be in enormous trouble with at least six of my mothers. "If my family finds out that I have been using my sword to hack at the heart of the Nine Realms—"

"Sif! Breathe!" Loki cuts me off before I can spiral. "Yggdrasil is enormous and as old as the universe. A few donks with an oversized knife won't hurt it."

She looks back toward the tree. "Besides, it wanted you here. That's kind of the deal . . . the World Tree is always paying attention."

Loki leans in close, and in the sly look

on her face, I suddenly get a glimpse of that trickster I had been warned about. "Doooooo you want to guess why the World Tree brought you here?"

"Because . . . I needed to meet you so that we could . . . I don't know, hang out?"

She looks shocked, then breaks out in a smile. "Yes, actually! That's it *exactly*. And since you're down here, I can show you my secret lair."

Secret lair? Is she really expecting me to get excited for a musty cave? Suddenly I'm thinking of all the things I should be doing with the rest of my day—write Mother a letter, comb the horses. . . .

And then I see where Loki's taken me. And . . . yeah, nope. I'm not doing any of that.

"We've got robots from Nidavellir! That drink machine? Always cold with ice from Jotunheim! The snacks? Toss 'em the hot box—it's filled with a little piece of Muspelheim I traded for a secret. And the best part of this place?"

"That's a very good rule." I smile. It *is* a pretty amazing lair. Pretty much the coolest lair I've ever seen, actually.

Loki gestures me over to the super-chill mushroom chairs. She sits down, and I follow. "Wait, no, this is the best part," she says.

"There's ANOTHER best part?" I'm still pretty overwhelmed at all the things I'm seeing that are already pretty much the absolute best.

"Oh yes. Right there." Loki points. "The crack in the roots just there, you see that? Gaze into it."

"Gaze?"

"Yeah. Just right into the roots. That light, just there."

I do. And what I see there takes my breath away.

I see a big white furry beast. He's got a little helmet and big pink eyes. And he's unlike any being I have ever seen. He is like a drawing, like one of my sketches, but he moves. And he's flying through the void of space, which should be impossible.

"I don't understand how the furry beast breathes," I say.

"He's Xemnu! He's from the Magic Planet!" says Loki, as if that explains anything. "Listen to the theme song, it explains everything." She puts a hand on my shoulder as she peers into the crack as well. "It's called 'television.' It's a completely useless collection of make-believe people acting like complete fools, but the people of Midgard can't look away."

"This is from Earth?"

"Yeah, 'Earth.' They make hundreds of hours of this stuff every week. If you look close enough, you can see scenes from all of Midgard's past, present, and even the future sometimes! And with that, every amazing bit of television they've ever produced. Midgard is, without question, the most ludicrous of all the realms." Loki sighs wistfully. "I can't wait to visit."

I press my eye back to the crack. I see a

man fighting with a monster, who is clearly just a man in a suit. And the fight is going so poorly that it looks more like a useless and clumsy dance.

"This makes no sense." I pull back from the crack. "It's like those two fighters didn't even *want* to kill one another."

"Exactly. It's all fake. Everything you see through the crack, it's just . . . stories."

"Stories from Midgard. Hardly the sagas of gods. Why do you watch this 'television'?"

Loki goes uncharacteristically silent. She takes a big breath. Maybe this was why Yggdrasil brought me here. Because Loki needed someone to talk to.

"I like that on Midgard, people have the option to be who they want to be," she says. "Not just a warrior, or a worker, or a god— they get to be who they really are. Some people start as peasants and become kings. Some start as kings and decide to be actors. And some just while away the hours, telling stories to unseen audiences. And, sure, there are plenty of Asgardians who get out of their stations . . . but not me. I can imagine a thousand lives for myself, but I'll never not be a child of Odin. I'll never not be royalty. No matter how little I might want to rule, I've got expectations. And living up to them doesn't always leave much room for living up to the me I want to be."

I put my hand close to hers. Close enough to let her know that she isn't alone.

And when I look back up, Loki's in boy form again. That same sly smile. That same twinkle in his eye.

I can't quite believe it, but after a day, where I watched my destiny get shattered . . .

. . . I think I've made a friend.

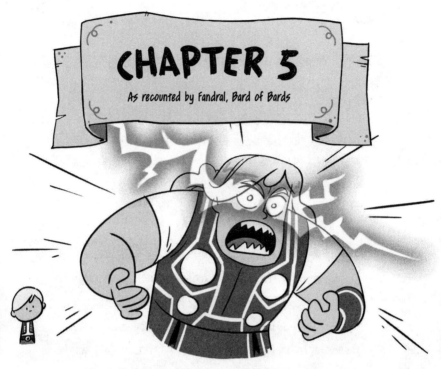

CHAPTER 5

As recounted by Fandral, Bard of Bards

"A babysitter?!?!? They think I need a
BABYSITTER?!?!?!?!?"

Thor's not a hard guy to read. When
he's upset, you basically know it from the
bulging eyes and the huffy breathing and the
extremely loud complaining. But there are
degrees of anger—just like there are degrees
of hot sauce—and you really only know
which level you're on by how and where Thor
chooses to throw his storm of a tantrum.

CATEGORY 1:
"THE BITTER BLIZZARD"

Nothing to worry about. These are generally just a bunch of pacing and pouting. They rarely make it farther than Odin's hall. Thor tends to run out of steam pretty quick on a Cat 1, so these storms usually defuse themselves.

CATEGORY 2:
"THE SULKY SNOWSTORM"

Big I'm-Going-to-My-Room energy. These are really only unfun for Thor himself, since he usually just disappears to his room alone for a couple hours. The door gets super cold and Thor gets super sad and honestly I mostly just worry about my good bud. But give him a few hours, show up with a kid-friendly root mead, offer him some mischief, and it's all good.

CATEGORY 3:
"THE DISPLEASED DOWNPOUR"

For these, I'm generally required. We go somewhere away from everyone else—like the Hall of Heroes or the Menagerie. His voice gets thundery, the air gets super wet, storm clouds brew, and sometimes there are tears. Never ever tell anyone I told you that, okay? Especially Thor.

CATEGORY 4:
"THE HUFFY HUFFY HURRICANE"

These tend to get pretty public and are almost always triggered by Odin yelling at Thor. My buddy goes absolutely bonkers, storming through the city and yelling at the sky. Structural damage to local buildings is a common side effect. I've had to tell that story everyone likes about how we met a lot during Cat 4s.

CATEGORY 5:
"THE TICKED-OFF TEMPEST!"

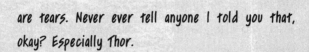

There's only one place Thor goes into full-on Cat 5 mode: Odin's Hall of Treasures.

Guess where we are right now?

Thor's already striding across the room, halfway to the Casket of Ancient Winters before I stop him.

"Thor! Come on, maybe it's nothing! Maybe Sif is secretly supercool? Like, she's from Vanaheim, right? They know a lot of awesome stuff in Vanaheim, they say the Old Gods have magicks and cool sword moves, and—"

KRAKABATHOOM

The whole place shakes. Which is saying something, because this "whole place" is hidden in a pocket dimension beneath the Great Palace of Asgard and really shouldn't be able to shake at all. Thor looks angrier than I've ever seen him. Normally it's just a THOOM or a KRAKATHOOM, but when it's a KRAKABATHOOM, you know you gotta be extra concerned.

"I don't want magicks, Fandral," Thor says quietly, which is somehow worse than when he's yelling. "I don't want cool sword tricks or new friends or assignments from my mother or lectures from my father. I don't want Loki laughing behind my back and you getting put down by my parents."

That last bit is kind of touching, actually.

"You and I spend every day training for the adventures I'll have in the future," he continues. "Sure, it's not the kind of training Sif does—it's more fun, it's less regimented, it's more *us*. But it's still preparing me to be what I need to be: a *hero*. And yet all my father ever seems to see is my failures. He'll never be proud of me if there's even a *chance* to be disappointed instead. He looks at all the cool stuff we do and what's his reaction? To give me a *minder*."

Thor looks down. Like he's embarrassed.

"He'll never see who I really am. Not unless I show him."

"That . . . makes sense," I say. "But how're you gonna get out of this whole arrangement if Odin won't even hear what you have to say?"

And that's when it shows up: The smile that says he's done with his Category 5 tantrum and has moved on to a little Category 10 Trouble.

"We're standing in his vault, Fandral."

"Yeah . . ."

"And what does my dad keep in his vault?"

"Treasures from across the Nine Realms?"

"*Super-powered* treasures from across the Nine Realms. The Casket of Ancient Winters can freeze a planet! The Warlock's Eye can control any mind! The Tuning Fork can, I dunno, tune a really big instrument?"

"Actually, legend says the Tuning Fork can reach beyond the dimensional rift and call forth the Lurking Unknown to destroy all of—"

"Whatever, Fandral. The point is it's powerful! Everything in here is *super-powerful*!"

"What are you getting at?" I ask. "Your logic is normally pretty straightforward but this particular lightning bolt is zigging and zagging a lot before hitting the target."

"I'm saying there's gotta be *something* in here that'll make Dad listen to me! All we have to do is find it!"

And that is how Thor and I find ourselves

raiding Odin's Vault—an activity strictly
forbidden by Odin himself under penalty of
Being Grounded for Literally All Eternity,
but desperate times call for desperate
measures. And if I'm being honest, by the
time we're done . . .

ENDANT OF
MYSTERY
Powers unknown,
presumed awesome

BRAGI'S HELM
Makes grumpy dads
listen to you.

. . . **we look good**.

"I'm going to use this magical helmet, and I'm gonna tell my dad that I don't *need* a babysitter," says Thor.

"Yeah, tell him!" I say.

"I'm gonna tell him I'm an adult!"

"A very young adult, but yeah, go off!"

"I'm gonna say, 'Dad, I'm ready for the battlefields of Muspelheim!'"

"Very cool— Wait. What?"

"'You can't keep me down anymore, Dad!'" Thor says, yelling at his imaginary Odin. "'I'm old enough to fight wars across the Nine Realms, face all kinds of untold dangers, finally make a name for myself. Hek, maybe I can even slay a dragon or two—'"

"I thought we were just saying something about Sif—"

"'—and Fandral's coming too!'"

"Wait. *What?*"

"Yeah! I'll tell him we're *both* old enough to go on adventures and be warriors and get glory for Asgard!"

"I mean, I still have a summer job. I'd have to ask my mom—"

"'And if you wanna fight me, Dad, you can *fight* me but I will lightning your butt across the room! Take THAT! HAH! CHAH! HAH CHAH!'"

Thor starts striking poses that really have nothing to do with convincing Odin of anything.

As we approach Odin's door, I start to seriously doubt our plan. We thought we'd walk right up and kick it open, and tell the old grump that we were done with his old-man face! But instead . . . we find that the door can't be kicked because it's already cracked just the littlest bit open. And behind it, hushed conversations.

Like, *secret* conversations.

I throw a hand over Thor's mouth and we both sidle up to the door to listen. Because whatever they're talking about in there sounds *important*.

So. You know. We snoop.

We snoop real good.

And what we hear changes our lives forever.

When Thor wants to do something, he moves like a strong gust of wind—and he tends to carry you right along with him. Which means that before I know it, I'm being pulled out of the Great Palace and into the streets of Upper Asgard by my very excited best-friend-in-arms.

"Did you hear that, Fandral?" says Thor. "This is **it!**"

"This is *what*?" I'm trying very hard not to face-plant while keeping up with Thor. "All I heard was some sad story about the Dark Star Something or Other—"

"Artifact! The Dark. Star. Artifact!" Thor emphasizes every word, like he's never heard three more beautiful sounds.

"And what's that supposed to be, exactly?"

"Who knows, Fandral?! And honestly, who cares? It's not about what it *is*; it's about the opportunity it affords the two of *us!*"

"What opportunity?" I pant. "Also, can we slow down? I didn't eat lunch, and this is all a little much."

"No! There's no time to slow down! We have to get to the Bifrost!"

I pull away. Getting dragged around Asgard is one thing. Getting dragged to the one place in Asgard we're *absolutely never allowed to go* is quite another.

"The Bifrost?! Thor, slow down for a second and tell me what the hek is going on in that big thundery head of yours!"

Thor stops and looks back at me. I swear I see little bolts of lightning come out the side of his eyes. That only happens when he's feeling extra hungry, extra angry . . .

. . . or extra awesome.

"Fandral," he says. "My friend. What's going through this thundery head is nothing less than our rise to the mantle of heroes. Asgard is in peril—her treasure has been taken from her, and my father can do nothing to stop it. Can't you see it?" he says as he claps a large hand on my shoulder. "It's our destiny to take up this challenge, travel to Nidavellir on our own, retrieve the Dark Star Artifact from

whatever heinous villain has spirited it away,
and then return it here to Asgard!" His eyes gleam
with excitement. He's really getting into this.
"Let's see my father try to give me some babysitter
when I've just rescued the very destiny of the
Nine Realms!"

I can't believe it either, but he's kinda selling
me on this.

"You're saying . . . you want to go on a quest?"

He smiles his perfect smile. I know there's no
getting out of this now.

"Not just any quest, Fandral. It's time for a . . ."

Hey, that'd make
a good title.

CHAPTER 6

A tale told by Sif, Warrior of the Vanir

We've been watching Midgard's finest television for several hours when Loki bolts out of his seat like a warcat called to battle.

"Oh, this is going to be *good*," my new friend mutters under his breath, clearly hearing or seeing something I can't. I doubt very much that he thought I could hear him—but he is a trickster, isn't he? Perhaps best not to make assumptions, lest they be the exact assumptions your trickster friend *wants* you to make.

"What's going to be good, Loki?"

He looks at me as if suddenly realizing I'm still here. His eyes are made of mischief.

"Oh, Sif. Daring, adventurous, quick-to-fight Sif. Now that I think of it, this should be rather good for you as well. So . . . perhaps it's best I just show you."

Loki knows all the shortcuts, so we make it from the edge of Yggdrasil all the way to the alleys of Lower Asgard in what feels like less than a minute.

He's clever and smart and especially brave for one known as a trickster. He transforms us both into all manner of forms as we go without hesitation. We become squirrels to run the roots of the tree, wolves to run across the rooftops, snakes to slither through the sewers, and even shadows to move through the darkness of the Low-Town alleys. With each new form comes a little sting of fear, but Loki's presence somehow comforts me.

They're so comfortable in every form. What I thought might feel strange instead feels liberating.

Wygul keeps up with us without transforming, of course, because he is a cat, and cats—the best of all animals—are blessed by Freya.

And at the end of the circuitous route, Loki leads me into an alley. He looks particularly antsy. Like a kid on Joltide morning, up way before the parents, just waiting for the festival to begin.

Which is when I realize I have no idea what time it is. Or how long I've been derelict in my Freya-given duties.

"Thor!" I exclaim.

"Not yet." Loki grins.

"What? I meant I was supposed to be

watching Thor and I completely lost track of time watching *The White-Thing's Magic Planet* with you!"

"His name's Xem—"

"I don't care what his name is, Loki! I came here to become a God of the pantheon of Odin, and here I am sneaking through alleys and ignoring my duties and bringing shame upon my family and I just—"

"Sif." Loki looks calm. Serene, even. And maybe an inch taller? "Everything is gonna be fine. You're closer to your duties than you think. Just walk out of the alley in five seconds. No more, no less. Got it?"

"Five seconds," I repeat, still pretty confused.

"Four now," says Loki, pushing me to the mouth of the alley.

"Three," I say.

"Two," he says.

We both inhale at the same time and simultaneously yell "ONE!" which gives me enough courage to step out of the alley to see whatever trick Loki's put in front of me . . .

which is when I see them. And I realize how
much of a friend Loki truly is.

"See what I mean?" Loki leans against the
alley. He looks particularly insufferable as a
boy. He must get it from his brother.

"Sif of the Vanir!" calls Thor. "If you think you're going to waylay us on our mighty quest, think again! I am Thor, son of Odin, and I'm going to—"

I have already stopped listening to his delusions of grandeur and his half-baked plan.

My mind is racing. Just hours ago, I was tasked with keeping this wayward prince on target. I was all but put in charge of his care, and by neglecting my duties for a single hour (or was it seven? Television makes time very blurry), I'd somehow given Thor a window to escape my watch and go . . . wherever he's going.

I remember how my third mother would react when I would disobey her orders and sneak into the woods to hunt lizard-rats in my younger days. How her voice shook the fear of Cul the Serpent into my very bones. How I'd do whatever she said when she was done raising her voice at me.

And so I reach deep into my chest and do the same to this tiny, petulant god.

HEAR MY WORDS, O SON OF ODIN! I AM NOT SOME CHILD OF THE OLD GODS FOR YOU TO ORDER ABOUT AND TREAT LIKE A CHAMBERMAID! I AM THE LADY SIF, GREATEST WARRIOR AMONG THE FREYAN OUTRIDERS, TRAINED IN THE METHODS OF WAR BY THOSE WHO PRAY TO YOUR MOTHER AND SHARPENED BY YEARS OF TRIALS! I KNOW MORE OF BATTLE THAN YOU COULD IMAGINE AND MORE OF DISCIPLINE THAN YOU WILL EVER GRASP. THERE'S MORE FIERCENESS IN MY CAT THAN THERE IS IN YOUR ENTIRE BODY! SO IF YOU THINK TO LECTURE ME, IT IS YOU WHO MUST THINK AGAIN!

I admit, I lost my temper a bit just there. Perhaps more than I ever have. Even Wygul looks a little shocked. Mother Above, I just yelled at a real-life god. And I must say.

It felt flippin' *great*.

For a moment, Thor just stands there. His fist is closed. His eye sparks with the power of his father's lightning. The distant thunder roils, no doubt at his subconscious command. I wonder if perhaps I've made a terrible mistake.

"I am burdened with heroic purpose. You are not going to stop me," says Thor.

I realize this may become a fight. Against a thunder god. And while I'm sure I could take him . . . I know it will not be pretty. And I doubt very much I will have a position in the palace by the end of the fight.

I have absolutely made a mistake.

But then, Loki steps in front of me, palms out and voice soft. "Thor. Brother. Don't you see what's happening here?"

"Of course I see, Loki," Thor replies, unmoving. Stern. "Just . . . tell me, anyway."

Loki throws his hand around Thor's shoulder. "Well, you seem quite loaded up for a quest," he says. "All the ravens, cats, rats, and little bugs in Asgard already know it—all but our father's eyes, the ravens Hugin and Munin. Those two birds watch everything in Asgard and would no doubt see you leaving—except of course that today Father's ravens have set their gaze on Alfheim due to reports slipped into their mind by a certain younger brother of yours. See, I know the Dark Star Artifact is missing. . . ."

Thor grabs Loki by the scruff of the neck. "What do you know of the Dark Star Artifact? Is this *your* doing, brother?!"

I instinctively reach for my sword—no boy will handle my only friend in Asgard like that—but Loki waves a small hand in my direction. *I've got this*, it seems to say.

"Thor, I'm an excellent prankster," says Loki. "I'll turn you into a frog all day long, but I'm afraid something so nefarious as stealing one of our father's greatest treasures from another realm entirely remains out of my reach."

Admitting a shortcoming seems distinctly un-Loki, which makes me think he has a plan.

"I'm not here to gloat," Loki continues. "I'm here to *help*. I want to retrieve the Dark Star Artifact alongside you and perhaps gain some small measure of trust from our stern patriarch. The halls of Nidavellir are dark and strange and full of all manner of dangers—you could use a crafty fellow like me to help you along. And what's more . . ."

Loki gestures to me, like a presenter on one of those Midgard shows he loves so well.

". . . I've brought you some *backup*."

I don't much love being referred to as *backup*, but I see what Loki's trying to pull. I also see how Thor's friend Fandral watches the interaction, waiting.

Slowly, Thor releases Loki. His gaze settles on me.

"Lady Sif. Do you . . . pledge your sword to me on this noble quest?"

"Um . . . what noble quest?" I say, genuinely confused.

"*Just say yes,*" whispers Loki. "*I'll fill you in along the way.*"

And so I look to Thor, remove my sword, and kneel begrudgingly before him. Technically, this was what Freya asked of me. Sort of.

"Your Highness. My blade is yours."

A long pause. I hope very much I am not about to feel the force of the lightning.

And then I hear his laugh.

"Hah! Good, then! Prepare yourself, Lady Sif, for we make for the Bifrost—and adventure!"

Thor walks ahead, and Fandral finally pipes up.

"Looks like this Thor Quest . . . just became a More Quest!"

He pauses for laughter but doesn't get any. I'm not sure I'll ever laugh at one of Fandral's jokes, and I think that speaks well of me.

Loki comes to me as I stand up, and takes my arm as we head toward the Bifrost.

CHAPTER 7

As recounted by Fandral, Bard of Bards

I need to take a minute here. Do you mind if we slow down? Because I think you need to understand something before we move into the next part of the story. We all know that the World Tree is this interconnecting magical force that unites all the realms. But it's an *actual* tree too—one that grows in Asgard, that extends gorgeous branches into each realm, etc.

But once you get onto the branches and

into the tree *between* the worlds? Things get a little weirder. Sure, there are branches that connect the realms, but they're hard to run along or really navigate the way you might in a tree—well, unless you're Ratatoskr the Omega-Squirrel.

See, the branches are spaceways made of time and stars and cool little nebula bits and reality barriers and occasionally a monster the size of several houses. But it's way easier to think of it as a tree, right? So we'll stick to that.

Okay, now that you understand the World Tree, this next bit starts to get weird again: the thing that DOES actually connect the realms? It's called the Bifrost, and it's a rainbow bridge.

I swear to you I'm not making this up; Asgard really is *that cool*.

The Bifrost is, predictably, a Pretty Big Deal. Without it, the only way between realms is the Cosmic Sea, but then you need a boat, and there's a lot of rowing, and I need to get real for just a moment: I am not really *built* for rowing.

Like all things that are a Pretty Big Deal in Asgard, the Bifrost has a guardian. Which is where our problem actually starts.

They call him . . .

The WATCHER of WAR!

THE GJALLARHORN GUARDIAN!

The man who's

NEVER LOST THE BIFROST!

The absolute

DEFENDER OF ASGARD'S ASSETS!

THE ONE!

THE ONLY . . .

HEIMDALL

"So, Thor . . . what're you going to do about Heimdall?" Loki says, cutting into my awesome Heimdall introduction.

Thor opens his mouth to say something that was going to be really clever . . . but then he closes it.

Loki rolls his eyes. "You don't have a plan, do you? You got so excited about getting here, you didn't even think far enough along to know how we were going to get past the God of Watching and Knowing Things."

He's being rude about it, but . . . Loki isn't *entirely* wrong.

"Just because you don't know my plan doesn't mean *I* don't know my plan," Thor says in a way that suggests he *obviously* has a plan. "And here is my plan. Which is the plan we will do. That I am going to say . . . now:

"I will challenge him to a holmgang."

Loki's mouth snaps shut. My jaw drops.

Holmgang?! It can't be a holmgang!

Let's get ready to RUMBLE!!!

HOLMGANG

A Holmgang is the ancient rite where two warriors have a duel for their honor. A duel . . . to the death!

So you can understand why we're all a little shocked.

It's Sif who breaks the silence, saying what we were all thinking: "Challenging Heimdall to a holmgang is like feeding yourself to an ice giant's even icier bear. It's like heroically sacrificing yourself at the end of an amazing story, except this is the beginning of the story, and so it isn't amazing in the least."

Reading the blank look on Thor's face, she sighs. "But you know what? I know you're not going to listen to me, so go ahead. When Heimdall knocks some sense into you, it is going to be *hilarious*."

Thor squares his shoulders, and in the distance, I hear a CRACK of thunder as he thunders, "Well, guess what? You're in luck because this is where the amazing *starts*. What's that? Oh, you're wondering what's about to happen? Thor—yeah, me, Thor—is going to go rock the Gjallarhorn Guardian so hard that the bards are going to call this HEIMDALL'S HUMBLING HOLMGANG!!!"

He half turns and shouts over his shoulder. "Tell 'em, Fandral!"

Oof. How am I going to put this to him? "Thor, that would be a very cool way to start the story, one hundred percent. But . . . it is going to be hard to back that story up if your head has been taken off your body . . . which is almost certainly what will happen if you holmgang against Heimdall."

The second CRACK of thunder tells me that was the wrong thing to say. Dang.

Thor plants his feet, and . . . well, sadly, I know exactly what my friend is thinking.

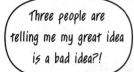

His knuckles curl around his ax, and I know, I KNOW, that Thor is about to go rushing off and there is literally nothing I can do to even think of stopping h—

"Okay, Thor, hold your holmgang," Sif says as she steps up to him, surprising both of us. "A few days ago, I would have been surprised that the Prince of Asgard would step into a duel he would absolutely lose in moments. Now, though? It's basically exactly what I expect. And keeping you from getting killed is *very specifically* one of the jobs your parents gave me. So . . . fine. I'll go distract him, and you three make your way to the bridge. Quietly."

Thor scoffs, "And how are you going to distract the man who can't be distracted?"

"Easy," she says. "He's my brother."

We all stare at her, blinking.

"What, you didn't know he was my brother?" she says, as if she hadn't just blown our minds. "Not that everyone from Vanaheim is related, but, well . . . we actually *are* related."

"But . . ." I could see the thoughts turning in my friend's head. "He is very cool. And you? Are . . . not so cool."

Sif raises a furious eyebrow. "Look, blondie, do you want me to go distract him or what?"

"Sif of the Vanir, you have come," says Heimdall, his voice rumbling through the air. So cool!

"Heimdall of the why are you talking like that? Stop being weird," she shouts back.

"I am not being 'weird,' little cat. This is what is expected of me now. Professionalism." The two of them approach each other . . . and sure enough, he's pretty dang distracted.

"You used to be funny."

"You used to be shorter."

"Okay, *big cat*, ha and ha," she says . . . and behind her back, she flicks her fingers. At us?

"*Moooooove*," Loki hisses, all but pushing us forward.

I start to move, Loki and Thor behind me. I've seen the Bifrost work a few times. As long as the sword is plugged in—which it is—all we have to do is turn it to Nidavellir and press GO.

"And how are our mothers?" I hear Heimdall ask.

"Good enough. Mama Iska has been raising a litter of Hel tigers, they're predictably both dangerous and adorable. Ma Rinari threw a spear that went all the way to Alfheim. And Mother Brun would very much like to know why you haven't written in two months?"

"I, uh . . ." Looks like the Watcher on the Wall didn't see that one coming. "I've been busy."

"Literally looking at nothing."

"Literally looking at all of reality."

I should in no way be surprised that Sif is great at irritating him. Siblings always have the perfect knack for driving each other crazy; look at Loki and Thor. If she can just keep it up for another few moments, we're almost to the sword. Thirty feet. Getting closer. Twenty feet. Just a little more—

"I can't take it," Thor says under his breath, ruining my hope of this actually working. "I can't stand this sneaking. Like, AT ALL. This is a total *Loki thing*."

Loki scowls. "Yes, it's a thing we do where you get what you want, rather than splattered against the floor."

"What was that?" says Heimdall, and for a moment, I'm positive we're toast. But as he starts to turn toward us, Sif cuts in with a "Hey! Did I tell you about Meema Sveld? She got an arrow to the knee!"

Heimdall sets his shoulders, and in that moment, he looks as stubborn as Thor. "Sif, it is really good seeing you, and let's gather again soon. But for now, the realms need my attention."

Across the room, I can see the panic in Sif's eyes. If she loses Heimdall's attention, we're *all* splattered against the floor. I turn to my best friend:

"Okay, here's how I see it. Most times? They're Thor Time. But sometimes? It's Loki Time. This sneaky shadow stuff? That can be Loki Time. Because then it gets us to the really awesome stuff, and that stuff? That's not just Thor Time . . . that's *Thor Time*."

Thor takes a frustratingly long moment to ungrip his ax. ". . . Verily. For now, it shall be . . . **Loki Time**."

I cut my eyes to Thor's brother. I'm not a huge fan, but the Heimdall situation is about to get out of hand unless someone has a big trick up their sleeve. And in my experience, like it or not, Loki is always the person with the biggest trick.

"I'll show you Loki Time,"

he mutters under his breath. His fingers flick and twist, glowing blue. For all of the cool stuff Thor and I get into, it's actually rare to see this kind of magic—it's not *not* cool. With a chop of Loki's hand, the magic winks out of existence, and the spell is cast. Whatever the spell is supposed to do . . .

"Heimdall! Show yourself!" thunders a voice from outside. Yeah, *thunders*. Somehow, ODIN HIMSELF is right outside?!

But even as Thor and I flinch, no one jumps higher than Heimdall. "The All-Father?!" he yelps, immediately looking to Sif. "You are not supposed to be here—"

"And I'm *already gone*, big brother. Just stall him out front. Give me a chance and I'll vanish, I swear."

Heimdall drops his massive hand onto his sister's shoulder. "Then be well, sister. We keep the tree."

"We keep the tree," I hear her say to his retreating back.

Loki pops up from hiding. "Sif, well handled! Boys, shall we?"

It suddenly dawns on Thor what is happening: "Very clever, Loki—I mean, I knew all along what you were doing but just now decided to tell you how clever it was that you feigned Father's voice."

"Well, it won't fool him long, so let's move!"

The four of us race to the great controls of the Bifrost. Thor grips the hilt of Heimdall's massive blade and uses his strength to twist the entire structure. Any of the realms could be our target, but Thor points us right to where we want to go.

Thor smiles to us, and I suddenly remember exactly why he's my best friend. "Is everyone ready for *adventure*?"

Loki says, "There's just no fun in stopping now."

"If you're going, I follow," says Sif reluctantly.

But me? I grin. "Hey, Thor, I seem to have lost my watch. Do you . . . know what time it is?"

CLICK!

Thor rests his hand on Heimdall's sword, knuckles turning white.

It's THOR TIME.

CHAPTER 8

A tale told by Sif, Warrior of the Vanir

We've been walking for less than half a day when I decide that this entire quest was a monumentally bad idea.

It turns out there is more to using the Bifrost than pointing the sword and holding on for dear life. As is seemingly always the case in Asgard, things are more complicated than the crown prince assumed them to be. Rather than being blasted directly to our destination on the wings of a mighty beam of pure light (as it was when I arrived from Vanaheim), when it comes to Nidavellir . . .

. . . it appears that we have to walk. All the way to another realm.

I suppose all I can say is that mistakes have been made.

The pace is quick—set by Thor, who is intent on leading the way. Wygul is perched gingerly on my head—why walk when you can ride?—and I try to make him proud by keeping up with Thor.

"Why don't you fall back and walk with my brother, Lady Sif?" Thor says beside me. "I'm sure his pace would be more to your liking."

"No, Prince Thor, I think I'll walk right where I am," I say as he matches me step for step. "I'm at the front, which is exactly where the leader should be."

"Ah, I see your mistake. It must be different back home. See, here in Asgard, the one who does the leading? That's the one who the quest is named for."

"Except"—I can't help myself—"we're not in Asgard."

"We're not anywhere," says Fandral, lagging behind. "We're nowhere! We're between where we've been and where we're going. On a bridge made of rainbow, between the stars and the Cosmic Sea!"

I can't see his point. "So?"

"So?" Fandral looks surprised. "I just . . . think it's neat."

The thing is, it *is* neat. Thor has been driving me so crazy, I haven't even taken the time to appreciate the fact that we're . . . well, we're walking through the universe. All the stars overhead, crisscrossed with neon nebulae. The sea below, tossed with wondrous waves. And us in the middle, on a bridge made of rainbows.

"It is neat," Thor says to me, his voice a reasonable level for once. "Sometimes Fandral is like that. You'll be all about this hyper-important thing, but then he shows up and he always makes sure you see the cool stuff."

Much louder, Thor says, "Great call, my dude!"

"I got you, bud!" Fandral yells back.

We walk along for another few minutes. Thor has stopped walking so hard. Now it's more like we were walking together, rather than racing for the lead.

I do not care for it.

"So," he says, "if I would have fought Heimdall. Well, I probably would have won. Obviously. But if I had lost . . . that would not have been great. Not saying that would have happened, but your plan . . ."

Why did I just say that? Obviously he would have lost, and obviously what I did was a good idea. I don't need his approval to do anything.

But this was his first attempt to actually say something nice to me. And it's not like we don't have men with overly large egos in Vanaheim—we ride lions for the Gods' sake—so that's not my real problem with him. My problem is that he instantly assumed I was useless, just because I was myself.

If he wants to correct that mistake? Back home, we have a saying: Don't stop sticking your face into the cat's soft belly just because they claw you in the head.

Translation: Everyone deserves a second chance.

"If I may interrupt your reveries, dear Sif and drear brother," Loki says, pointing up at the sky. "I believe we are about to be hit by a meteor."

Wait. We're about to be hit by a what?!

A METEOR?!!!

Truly, I think, a bad idea.

We plunge into the icy water below, sinking like stones. But also, falling upward in an experience that feels as strange to endure as it does to talk about. I see Fandral and Thor both turning red as they hold their breath, but I know it's just a matter of time before we all have no choice but to breathe in the salty brine. Well, except for Loki. Loki has turned into a fish.

I feel Wygul's claws digging into my skin. A cat in the water, I can only imagine how much he is hating this . . . but when I look down, he just looks back.

"Meooooooow," he says. He says? We're underwater; he shouldn't be able to talk. Talking requires air, which . . .

Swim   Swim

". . . should be impossible," I say.

Thor, fish-Loki, and Fandral all share a look, and Loki turns back into their female human form. The three all breathe in the water . . . which is also, somehow, oxygen. As if any of this could get any stranger.

"Um, Thor?" Fandral says, pointing down. "Or Loki, or Sif, or . . . anyone? The water below is . . . turning darker."

Loki rolls her eyes. "Fandral, you sweet bean, I think you mean to say that the water below us is dark. Which is how water works."

"Except I don't mean that, because I know how water works, and it is actively changing color toward the darker end of the spectrum. Like, right now. I'm watching it happen."

I look down, and see that the bard isn't entirely wrong. Below us, the water is getting darker. With little white edges. Or actually, pretty big white edges. Rapidly growing white edges that look kind of like teeth. Which doesn't make any sense, because each of those teeth would need to be . . . I mean, they would need to be the size of . . .

And in a flash, I know exactly what I'm looking at:

"SEA SERPENT!!!"

At the last moment, the creature SNAPS its jaws shut, snaking past and sending us end over end in the water. As it passes, I can see its eye looking straight at us—an eye as big as Freya's chariot. Attached to a head bigger than the body of the largest frost giant. Connected to a body . . . that vanishes into the depths below.

A beast this big isn't "just" a sea serpent. There is only one beast this large in all the Nine Realms. Only one dragon large enough to encircle the world . . .

JORMUNGAND!

"THAT IS CORRECT, CHILD OF
THE VANIR. IT IS I, JORMUNGAND.
THE SERPENT THAT ENCIRCLES THE
WORLD."

"Wow" the three others say in unison.
So helpful.

"Great Jormungand," I say, desperately
trying to think of how we can survive this. "We
beg you to . . . not eat us. We would . . . really
appreciate that."

In an uninspiring vote of no confidence,
Wygul hides behind me—even a warcat has
trouble with a super-serpent.

"EAT YOU? NAWWWWW, GIRL. YOU
FIVE ARE NOT EVEN WORTH IT. YOU'RE,
LIKE, NOT EVEN A MOUTHFUL. TOTALLY
INSIGNIFICANT, REALLY."

"Insignificant?!" Oh lords, here Thor
goes. "I am Thor! Prince of Asgard, Herald of
Thunder! I would make a magnificent meal!"

"NOPE."

"It would be glorious to eat me!"

"NAW."

". . . Why not?"

"THE GODLING FINALLY ASKS A QUESTION WORTH ASKING. BEYOND THE TRICKSTER, I SEE FANDRAL, LADY SIF, AND THOR. THREE WARRIORS . . . BUT NOT THE WARRIORS THREE."

I'm confused, but Jormungand presses on. "ONE DAY, THUNDER GOD, WE SHALL MEET. AT RAGNAROK, AT THE END OF THE WORLD. THAT IS WHEN I SHALL EAT YOU. DOES IT LOOK LIKE TODAY IS RAGNAROK?"

". . . No?"

"THEN YOU ARE NOT ON THE MENU. YOUR JOURNEY HAS JUST BEGUN."

"So . . ." Thor says, and I genuinely wish he would just stay quiet. "You can see the future?" The serpent looks on knowingly. Thor continues, because apparently knowing when to stop is not a godly virtue. "If you can see the future, you have to tell us what happens next! That's just how it is, I don't make the rules!!!"

"THOR, YOU ARE SUPER BUMMING ME OUT WITH THIS. I'M KIND OF DONE TALKING TO YOU NOW.

"I SHALL ONLY TALK TO MY FATHER.

"I SHALL ONLY TALK . . . TO LOKI."

Loki?! We all turn to her, and she just looks back at us, equally confused. But then her face gets cross, and I start to see the same kind of look that I've seen on Thor: trouble.

"Okay, big guy, listen to this. No one tells me what I am or amn't. I'm Loki, I'm me, and I am certainly not your dad."

"AND YET, YOU ARE. IN THE SEA OF SPACE, THE CURRENT OF TIME PULLS IN ALL DIRECTIONS."

I've spent enough time with the Vanir soothsayers to know that means, *Don't try to think about it too much. It'll just hurt your brain.*

"Loki, hey. Hey, Loki. Hey." Thor swims closer to Loki, whispering. "If this thing thinks you're its dad, maybe it can get us to Nidavellir? Just like . . . do a little tricky trick?"

"I don't do 'tricky tricks,' brother," Loki whispers back. "But yeah, maybe I can work with this. Give me the helmet you stole. Fandral, the necklace too."

"What? Haha. We didn't steal a—"

"*Thor.*"

"Yeah, fine," he says, handing the helmet over (Where was he hiding that thing?) while Fandral digs out the necklace. Loki takes them both . . . and puts the helmet on her head.

"Oh, great Jormungand! My great big scaly child!" Loki bellows.

"Hear me now!"

Loki's voice bellows through the water, and the serpent gives her all the attention.

"My companions and I seek the realm of the Dwarves, in their great metal halls. If you would take us there, great riches could be yours!"

". . . FOR REAL? I LOVE SOME GREAT RICHES."

"Totally! When we get to Nidavellir, the most riches. And in good faith, let us give this to you now. This . . . really cool necklace!" Loki pulls a necklace from Fandral's bag. It looks pretty fancy.

". . . WHAT'S IT DO?"

"Psst, Fandral," Loki says quietly. "What's it do?"

"No idea."

"You stole a magical necklace and you don't know what it does?"

"Yeah, we're just cool like that."

"UGHHHHH," Loki and I both groan.

"YOU KNOW WHAT? I'M IN. HAVEN'T BEEN THAT WAY IN A WHILE, MIGHT BE COOL. SO YEAH, JUST PUT THAT SWAG RIGHT ON MY BIG OL' TOOTH."

Swimming close, Loki hangs the glittering necklace from the world serpent's fang . . .

. . . and a SHOCK runs through the massive wyrm's body. And his eyes turn ANGRY.

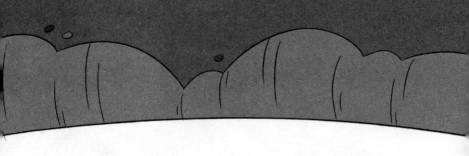

Wow, what is with today and bad ideas?

"YOU SEEK TO IMPRISON JORMUNGAND?! YOU USE DARK-ELF MAGIC TO BIND ME TO THE DEPTHS?!"

"Eeeshhhh," mumbles Thor. "You know, now that I'm really thinking about it, I *do* think that necklace was a gift from the Dark Elf King Malekith the Accursed, potentially designed to take control of Dad's mind to do evil?? Which is why Dad kept it locked up and didn't wear it. So you know what? This one is on me."

Fandral looks appalled. "Thor, I wore that necklace!"

"I said potentially."

"DEATH TO THE FATHER! DEATH TO ALL!"

Thor draws his ax. Does the fool think he could fight this thing?! "Get behind me! And as soon as you can, grab on to his head!"

With a coiling rush, the massive serpent charges right for us. . . .

As the creature misses us, Loki, Fandral, and I grab on to the scales just behind his head, and Wygul grabs on to me.

Instantly, we start moving faster than anything should be able to move. As fast as a storm! As fast . . .

. . . as lightning.

Into the water, out of the water, the great dragon dives and surfaces like a mustang trying to throw its rider. But the five of us cling to its massive scales, our hands working into the crevices to hold on.

"Thor, stop!" cries Loki. "We can hide! We can run!"

"No, sibling!" bellows Thor. "We must fight!"

BOOM BOOM BOOM BOOM!

With every swing of his ax, another bolt of lightning slams into the dragon's head, and I realize, Thor isn't just fighting. . . .

He's "steering" the serpent . . . *Straight toward Nidavellir!!!*

Up ahead, I can see a massive maelstrom of water—the boundary between the Cosmic Sea and the realm of the Dwarves.

"Loki, Fandral, Sif, Cat! Get ready to jump! There's a waterspout up ahead—if we can all throw ourselves into it, it'll launch us the rest of the way!"

"This idea is very poor!" screams Loki.

"No . . ." Fandral says, grinning. "This idea is very *Thor*!"

Across the beast's head, Thor and I lock eyes. "Lady Sif! Do it now!"

"FOR VANAHEIM!" I yell as *I donk the big snake with my sword*!

And as the massive dragon WHIPS his body around, the five of us JUMP . . .

. . . sailing toward the maelstrom wall, the storm of storms . . .

. . . SLAMMING INTO IT AT FULL SPEED . . .

DONK!

WHIPS!

JUMP!

SLAM!

DARKNESS!

And then everything goes black.

CHAPTER 9

I'm cold.

I'm cold and I hurt.

I'm cold and I hurt and I'm . . .

. . . alive?!

"I would like to inform everyone," I groan with joy, "that we are, in a surprising turn of events, not at all dead."

"How lucky for us," Loki mumbles as he picks himself up from the snow. Wait, snow?

Fluffy, white, a little bit of crunch under my fingers. Yep, this is snow. "This is snow," I say, because apparently my clever word powers got knocked out of me for what I can only hope is a blessedly short time.

"Fandral," Thor says, "I'm sorry to say this, but you're wrong. This isn't snow . . ."

IT'S ADVENTURE!!!

My eyes scan the landscape. All the snow and ice, stretching to the horizon . . . did we land in Jotunheim? I am not *big* on meeting any frost giants. . . . I mean, I don't have a *large* interest in . . . come on, Fandral. This is no time for puns. Pull it together—

"The great Dwarvish mountains of Nidavellir," says Sif . . . and I knew that. Obviously. Who's afraid of frost giants? Not this guy. "Grown from the fallen warriors of the ancient Dwarves, who towered over all but Yggdrasil herself. Their ancestor Dwarves live beneath the surface and fill the realm with the works of their mighty forges. See, look beyond that ridge . . ." Sif points. "Those are giant vents. And those trees? You can tell that they're made of metal."

Looking closer, I see she's absolutely right. Underneath the snow, it's not dirt and woods—it's vents and gears and brass pipes and connecty bits! This is an entire mechanical world!

I catch Thor's eye as he tries to catch my eye. And suddenly—

"Thank you, Sif, for explaining the obvious," Thor says, stepping forward with style. "I got us here . . . but now we need to find how to get inside. To *the caverns*. Which are *under us*." He gives me a wink and a small thumbs-up.

"Thor . . ." says Sif, clearly ready to snap back at him. But then . . . she doesn't. "That's a good call, actually. Let's split up and cover more ground, but keep someone in sight at all times! Watch your feet to avoid holes—"

"Unless it's a safe hole," says Loki.

"Yes, unless it's a safe hole," Sif repeats. "And if you see something, give two squawks like a fire heron, but three squawks if you've lost sight of . . . Oh, you're all gone. . . ." Her voice fades, trailing off as we all strike out in different directions, eager to find a way inside.

As I crest a small rise, my foot slips on a patch of ice. I not only fall on my butt, but I slide down the short slope, farther from the rest of the group. I brush the snow aside, and underneath is densely packed coils of metal pipe, woven together like a bird's nest, or a spider's cocoon. Yeah . . . we're not getting in this way.

I stand up, dusting myself off, and see a short kind of smokestack ahead of me. Except . . . no smoke is coming out. Which seems odd. And so, I get curious. I rush over and start whacking it to remove some of the snow.

And there, I find a door.

I give two squawks like a fire heron, because of course I was listening to Sif. She's annoying but also very clever.

While the others assemble, I manage to get the door open. Inside isn't a stairway, but a little room, with up and down arrows. Which I don't have to tell you is pretty weird, because little rooms don't go up and down?

GOES DOWN?

how do they do that?

"Good work, Fandral!" says Thor, clapping me on the back. "It looks like there's only room for two, so . . . sorry, Sif and Loki. The Warriors Two will go ahead and—"

"No, no," says Sif. "Thor, you're too . . . important to go first. What if it's dangerous? Stay here with Fandral and Loki and I will go on down and—"

Loki cuts in, "I don't actually want to go first? Someone else should go do the dangerous stuff."

Well, I love the dangerous stuff!

As Thor and Sif vanish into the magical moving room . . .

Dude, I'll miss you.

Bro, same.

Try not to kill Sif.

Feel free to kill Loki.

Now I'm waiting with Loki. Time is dragging to a near standstill, it's been . . . at least twenty minutes.

"This is the longest four minutes of my life," says Loki. "Please, Fandral, say something funny."

"I have nothing funny to say to you." And I don't. Talking to Loki isn't worth the stress. I'm just going to stand here and not say anything. Deal with that.

"So now you're not going to say anything, hrm? Ah yes, something you and I have in common: our famous ability to keep our mouths shut."

I'll show him who can't keep his mouth shut! "You know, for someone who can be anything, it's wild to me that you choose to be a *jerk*. All you've done since we started is drag your feet and snipe and be a real pain in the—"

"Excuse me? 'All I've done'?! Right, I forgot—Heimdall caught us, and the sea serpent ate us. Oh, wait! That's two saving-the-day points for me, and let's see. Brave Fandral has . . . zero saving-the-day points? Well, shoot, that's too bad. How many points do you think you get for 'found a door'?"

"See? This is what I'm talking about! Right here! You're being a real pain in the—"

"Say it!"

"A real pain in the ax."

That shuts Loki up, for just a beat. And then . . . he smiles. Kind of. So do I, actually.

"See, I knew you had something funny to say."

After that, we both exhale a little bit.

Loosen up. Because honestly, who knows how long we'll be waiting.

So we just chill. And watch the snow.

When the magic box—sorry, Loki called it an "elevator"—opens again, Thor and Sif are gone and it is our turn.

Climbing in, the door slides closed with a little *thonk*, and then a *ding*—and the whole room shakes. But I am very cool about it and not at all surprised.

"Fandral," Loki says, for once not using his kind of weird slimy tricky voice, "can I ask you a question? Like, a genuine question, that you can totally not answer?"

Rare to get this kind of honesty from Loki. Might as well see where it leads. "Sure."

He works really hard to avoid eye contact with me. "What do you get out of being Thor's friend?"

"What?" I scoff. "I get to be friends with Thor. That's its own reward."

"No, see, you just did it again. A friend makes you happy, or glad, or mad, or whatever. The reward for friendship should be friendship, not 'getting to be friends.'"

"Loki . . . look." Jeez, strong start, Fandral. Be careful with what you say here because Loki is going to twist it up real good. "A lot of people think that Thor is . . . self-centered. They think that he's dense, and selfish, and, I don't know, other not very nice things that they whisper when he's not listening. But I hear them because . . . well, when he's around, I'm harder to see. The thing is, though, he's self-centered because . . . well, he's the center. He's the prince, he's heroic, he's kind and cool and he's honest—"

"He lies *literally* all the time."

"But never about anything that matters." I kind of lapse for a second. I'm not explaining this right, but at least Loki isn't cutting me off again: "He's the center because . . . he holds things together."

He's really giving me the time to explain myself. Or time to put my foot in my mouth.

But I take it because, honestly . . . it feels
really good to talk to someone.

"What do I get out of his friendship?
I get to help him be his best self when he
doesn't quite know how. That's better for, well,
everyone. I help him, and he helps the world.
It might not be a normal kind of friendship,
but it's the kind we have. And
. . . it's enough for me. And I know it's
enough for him."

Loki doesn't say anything for a long
moment. And then . . . "Thank you for sharing
that. I . . . guess I didn't see it that way."

Once again, we stand in silence.

"Can I ask you a question?" I ask after a
long moment, which I know is technically a
question already but I hope Loki just lets
it slide.

"Seems fair."

"Do you have any idea what the Dark Star
Artifact actually is?"

Loki snorts. "Not in the least. I asked
around, even read some diaries, but Odin and
Freya might be the only ones who know.

Well, and the Dwarves. Luckily, we don't need to know what it is . . ."

He claps his hands together, and between them bursts a bright light! As he slowly pulls his hands apart, wiggling his fingers in a way that looks just a little bit silly, he creates a magical sigil that hangs in the air. In the center of it is an arrow, pointing off in a direction away from us.

". . . in order to find it!"

As the door *dings*, I smile at Loki's showmanship—gotta respect the craft. "A

 world to explore and some magic to point the way? Loki . . . I think, for the first time, that we might actually have things under control."

And then the doors open, and I realize immediately:

 we do not.

CHAPTER 10

A tale told by Sif, Warrior of the Vanir

I step into the magical transportation room, and Thor follows. The door closes with a little *thonk*, and then a *ding*—and the whole room shakes. But I am very cool about it and not at all surprised.

The room is big enough for two, but Thor somehow seems to take up more than half the space. How can one person be so big when he is categorically smaller than me?

"Magic box go down?" Thor muses. "Very neat."

"I'm sorry, are you trying to start a chat? About our mode of transportation?"

"I was, actually. Yes, good of you to notice. Quite an honor to small talk with Thor. I said that it's very neat."

This fool. He genuinely doesn't know the difference between magic and a system of rudimentary pullies. I guess he isn't the God of Brainstorms. "It's not a magic box, Thor. I can hear gears behind the walls—I imagine it's some kind of mechanization."

"Well . . ." Thor says, with a pondering look on his face. "Odin says that magic and science are basically the same thing, so . . . are you saying that the All-Father is wrong?" And he grins, like he just won a point.

I grind my teeth. Of course I wouldn't, and he knows that. He laid a trap for me, a trap of words— and I stepped right in it. The fool. Laid a trap. For me. But to think that I would be so immature as to be keeping some kind of score in my head regarding our conversations is ridiculous.

Go team ThorQuest!

SIF VS THOR
38   6

"Hey, Sif?" he says, his voice pitched at just that incredibly annoying tone of voice. "You look pretty upset. . . . Are you okay?"

He dares? He dares ask Sif of the Vanir if she is okay?!

"Of course I'm okay!" I yell.

He looks at me—and in his shock, I see myself. That was . . . not a proportionate response.

I'm...a little anxious.

Even as I say it, I want to take it back. If this is another word trap he's setting for me, I'm going to show him what happens when you wake a sleeping lioness. It involves claws.

"We're descending into the unknown. Searching for something that Odin himself couldn't acquire, without any more information than its name. About to step foot inside a strange realm, full of people who . . . aren't our enemies, but aren't necessarily our friends. And who, if they don't kill us, will almost certainly report us back to your parents."

Thor looks aghast. "They wouldn't *dare.* Not if I told them not to. They'd get me in so much trouble!"

"Thor, we're not in Asgard. You're the son of a King who the Dwarves don't actually like that much." I push back some of my hair that escaped the braid. "And once we're caught, you'll be, what, grounded? But if I fail . . ."

The words are pouring out of me, like a sudden flood of things that I have very tactfully not been saying. "I would lose my honor. Do you get that? You have this quest you've made for yourself, but I've already been given a quest by the Queen and King of the Gods: to keep you safe, and keep you out of trouble."

He keeps his mouth shut for once. Could he have actually heard me?

And then we both hear a SPINE-SHAKING YOWL—

—and Wygul launches himself into Thor's arms, glaring at me with a look that says:

Girl, you didn't even know I was here. Well guess what—you can't forget me now.

Because I'm here.

Star of the show.

Wygul Quest.

"I guess he likes me?" Thor grins, five pounds of smug feline in his arms.

"Of course he does," I can't help but say. "Everyone likes you. That's kind of your *whole deal*."

"Oh." I can tell he's actually caught off guard by what I guess he thinks is a compliment. "Thanks?

". . . Does that mean you like me?"

Luckily the door *dings*, and I don't have to answer that.

Thor and I step out of the up-and-down room, and we're both struck quiet. Partially because of the silence we've stepped into, the kind of silence that only happens in between glaciers or in huge empty mead halls. An echoing kind of silence that fills the tunnel we're now standing in.

"Tunnel" is probably a bad word for it— super-sized tunnel? No wait, Jormungand-sized tunnel. Wide enough for the great serpent himself to swim through. Vast. And every inch made out of twisting pistons and brass tubes. Some part of me can't believe we're really here, but now it couldn't be clearer.

We've made it.

NIDAVELLIR
Realm of the Dwarves

When Thor speaks, it's just above a whisper. Even he is awestruck by this place.

"You know, Sif," he says, "I really heard what you said in there. About your quest. And your honor. I really get that. I mean, sure, I like being liked but . . . honor. Really, that's my thing too."

I frown, trying to figure out where this is going.

"'Keeping me safe'?" he says, clearly having some difficulty navigating the words he was trying to say. "I don't think I really need it, but sometimes . . . Fandral needs a hand. So, I've decided I'm fine with it."

He straightens, shoulders back, like he's preparing for something. "Keeping me out of trouble though? I'm afraid that's gonna be harder."

That pompous little—

"You're going to want to turn around."

Only then do I realize that I've been captivated by what I could see down the forever tunnel.

Forever Tunnel, that's what I should have

called it. Anyway, I was looking one way. Which means . . . well, which means I hadn't turned to see what was in the other direction. The direction Thor's looking.

"So, do you think it's a machine?" Thor says, his voice shockingly steady.

I draw my sword, and see Wygul wisely stick himself into a safe little spot. "I do, yeah."

"Excellent," Thor says, flipping his ax into his hand like he's about to chop some wood. "Have at thee!!!" he thunders as he leaps toward the monster!

"ROOOARR!" it bellows back!

"For Freya!" I scream, breaking to the right as Thor runs left. Because of course

I'm going to fight—the epic they write about this will be legendary, and I'll not have history think that Sif stood by and watched!

I leap onto the metallic beast's back as Thor grabs on to its metal jaws. Our weapons slam down into its metal hide, which is as thick as any armor. No fight is over after the first blow, and I know in my heart:

I will not fail.

But across the tunnel, I *do* miss the sound of a *ding*. The magic box once again opens and, well . . .

...ah dang

CHAPTER 11

As recounted by Fandral, Bard of Bards

A little help here?

Feelings are weird beasts. The older folks always tell you to control them, to manage them, to be the master of your own emotions. But in my experience, most feelings don't work like that. Most feelings you feel no matter what. And when you feel them, you react.

When a giant spider shows up, I get afraid (even if it's the friendly one named Spooder that lives down the street).

When the Asgardian fencing squad takes first in the Realmic Leikmót, I get psyched (and I'm gonna make the team someday, just you watch).

When Loki shows up, I get suspicious. Because that's just what you do.

So I have no choice in what transpires next. I really don't.

Because someone is picking on my best friend.

I *feel* it . . .

. . . so I react.

"Hold on, Thor!" I shout as I leap toward the Dwarven construct! Its roar sends booming echoes through the caverns with breathtaking force, a perhaps-too-obvious warning to all predators to stay away lest they be chomped in metal jaws and trampled underfoot. And yet here I am, stabbing my rapier into the inch-long space between its robotic femur and its metallic meniscus.

Is this what being a hero feels like? Because it feels *good*.

"What are you doing, Fandral?" shouts Sif. She sounds annoyed—surprise, surprise. I'm starting to believe she could be annoyed by *anything*. "Who trained you in the ways of war?!" She scoffs. "A sporting blade isn't going to do anything against an opponent of this caliber! Stop stabbing and find another way to help!"

She's underestimating me. She has no idea. Pride swells in my chest. This will be fun.

"But that's just the thing, Lady Sif." I smile at her, my best charmer's smile. "I'm not stabbing."

I place my foot on the hilt of my sword, bending it down. The metal curves beautifully—tense with energy. Waiting for release, held down only by my body weight.

"What *are* you doing, then?"

I wink.

"Making leverage."

I step onto the blade . . . and it launches me at least a hundred feet in the air!

Sif's eyes, rightfully astonished, follow me the whole way up. It's absolutely the coolest thing I've done this week. Maybe this year. Maybe ever.

Maybe going on an ill-advised adventure wasn't so ill after all.

I land atop the beast's back, just a short sprint from its neck—and there I can see Thor, holding on to the creature's head! The beast is thrashing and bashing to get Thor off—but he's gripped tight to the back with all the strength of an Asgardian!

"Thor!" I yell. "Grab my hand!"

"Nay, Fandral! If this thing wants me off, let it dash its own head against the wall first!"

Did he just say "nay"? And is he making his voice deeper on purpose? I suspect he's trying to sound like a hero from the sagas. And I gotta say, he's kind of pulling it off. Good for Thor.

"This strategy is madness, Thunder God!"

shouts Sif—who makes Thor's hero voice sound practically rehearsed. "You'll be dashed along with the creature! Leave the tactics to me. In the Freyan Outriders, I'm known as the—"

BAM. THWACK. SMASH. BOOM. THUD.

So. Less-than-good update.

The beast does exactly what Thor hoped—HEADBUTTING the ground. And it's exactly as much of a bad idea as Sif said. 'Cause, see, turns out, the big metal monster can take a hit to the head. Thor? Less so. My best bud looks dazed. And that's before the Mecha-saurus kicks him across the room and into a pile of gears, which then explode.

That's gonna leave a mark.

Sif lifts her blade, ready to make a mark of her own on the T-RoboRex's hide, when the newly freed beast sees her and, with a single swift kick, knocks Lady Sif all the way across the tunnel. A second THUD, just for good measure.

It's a wild display. So wild, I don't even realize the truth until it's too late: I'm now standing alone on top of the back of a mechanical dinosaur and all I've got to fight with is a kind of bent rapier.

I look down at my thin sword and practically will it to, just this once, be a longsword or an ax or a hammer—hek, even a really heavy fish would do. Anything but this, a pointy stick that's barely even pointy. But it doesn't change.

The metal monster turns its neck to look at me. Its clockwork eyes peer into my soul.

And that's when I hear Loki.

"Lovely work, Fandral. Quite the distraction."

My mind—as if on instinct—races as soon as I see Loki's grin. His smile is usually accompanied with a trick, a joke, a jape, a lie, or, in worst cases, a prank.

I even keep an ongoing list of his most infamous achievements, just as an insurance policy that we won't fall for them again. Thor calls it THE MANY REASONS WHY MY BROTHER IS THE WORST, but I call it my . . .

LOKI FILE!

№ 196:

Loki plants carnivorous plants in the palace garden. Thor is eaten. Twice.

Recommendation: No more garden walks.

№ 252:

Loki shape-shifts into a fish. Lures Thor to nearby lake with promises of Fish Treasure. When Thor is at edge of lake, Loki pulls Thor in and ruins Thor's favorite tunic.

Recommendation: No more believing fish.

№ 616:

Loki distracts Thor during breakfast, swaps their plates, eats Thor's breakfast.

Recommendation: No more breakfast.

VETO, FANDRAL! I'M NOT LETTING LOKI TAKE BREAKFAST FROM ME!

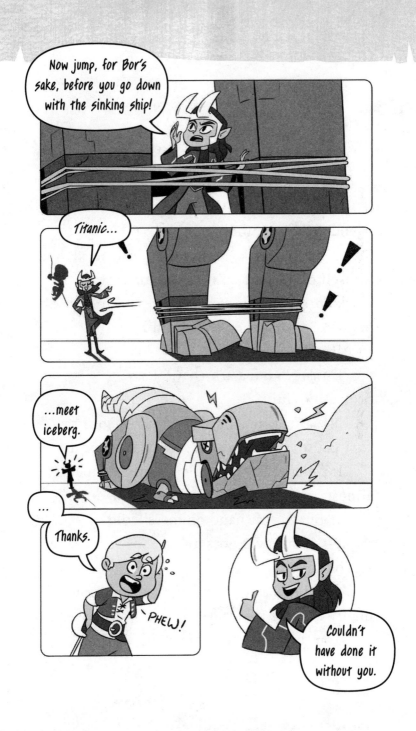

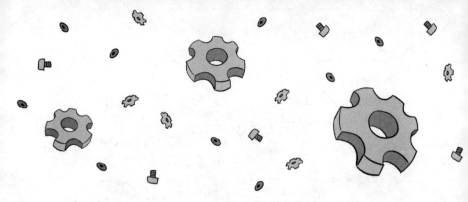

And yet here he is, looking at me like a friend. Like a teammate.

"Before you ask," says Loki, dusting himself off, "I had no idea the giant clockwork monster would be here. I'm not behind every wicked plot from here to Alfheim."

"I wasn't gonna ask that," I say, probably lying.

"No. But you thought it. Just then. I saw."

I pause, speechless. Which is new for me.

"It's okay." Loki's smile becomes somehow almost imperceptibly sad. "Everyone does."

He puts a soft hand on my shoulder. The sadness in his eyes goes away. "We still make a good team."

And then he turns to help Sif, who's just finally getting to her feet.

"You might want to check on my brother,

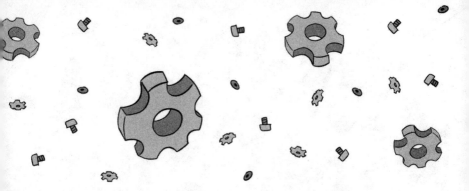

Fandral," he says. "I think he got a tad exploded."

Loki steps away, helping Sif up (even though it's clear she doesn't want any help). I know I should turn and go help Thor, but I'm still trying to work out whether Loki was just trying to get into my head. Or did we really just take down a monster together and all he was trying to say was *Good job, Fandral. We should hunt more monsters together*? Or maybe this is some kind of weird plan to turn me against Thor?

Dang, friends. Adventures are confusing.

They're also *dangerous*, even when they seem like they're not. Especially when they seem like they're not.

Case in point: that monster we just took down, the Mecha-saurus? Well, guess what?

Now it's . . .

I stare up at the creature, unable to move. Next to me, Sif and Loki. Both similarly stunned into stillness.

"You got a plan for this, princess?" I mutter to Sif.

"I do not," she says. "But if you call me 'princess' again, the plan's going to be feeding you to that thing while we run away."

"Guys," says Loki, eyes still on the Largest Beast Any of Us Have Ever Seen. "Might I remind you: priorities."

The creature turns its huge eight-eyed face toward us. Its jaws open, large enough to swallow any of us whole. I imagine a hundred scenarios where we fight—and in every one, we get eaten. I consider what kind of flashy story or song might convince the beast to leave us alone, but I don't suppose spider-dinosaur nightmares are much known for their love of verse.

"Loki, you must know another trick. Perhaps it's got an off switch?"

Loki looks at me like I'm the biggest dingus alive.

"Right. No off switch. Makes sense."

I realize now that this might be the end for me.

And it's a terrible ending. Just dreadful.

The beast rears back.

I close my eyes.

And I hear the very last thing I expect.

Thor leaps at the Arachno-Mega-Mecha-saurus with a charge of thunder so powerful it makes the room tremble! Sif covers her ears—she's not used to the might of the Aesir, but this will show her all she needs to see.

Thor might be a big lug sometimes, but he's got more power in his pinkie than 99 percent of the creatures in all the realms in all of existence. He's an elder god-in-waiting—the All-Father's true heir—and his body courses with the very heart of every storm that ever was and ever shall be. It takes a lot out of him to use it, but it's always there, right beneath the surface. His eyes are actually lightning and his voice is actually thunder and his hair is actually that luxurious. He's not a kid playing at being a big, important god, like me and Sif and (mostly) Loki.

He's the Actual God of Thunder.

And when he decides to show it off, the best thing to do is stay out of his way.

The Arachno-Mega-Mecha-saurus learns this the hard way.

Thor's energy courses through the beast's metal body with a single incredible punch—sending it flying across the tunnel! It SLAMS into the wall and BANGS into the floor, and Thor SMASHES it up into the ceiling and then THROWS it against the far wall. He unleashes a wild torrent of electricity across the hall, and several more scrap piles explode!

"Get down!" screams Sif as she reaches her blade up to catch a piece of incoming debris in midair. Her cat—I think his name is Weevle?—leaps onto my shoulder and digs his claws in for stability.

The Spidersaurus-Rex roars a final bellowing HOWL into the ancient corridors, all anger and rust and just a little bit of surprise.

And then Thor's lightning fist KRA-KOOMS its mecha-head RIGHT OFF ITS ROBO-BODY!

I can barely see through all the dust and smoke, but I hear the beast fall for a final time.

The fight is over.

"No need to thank me," says Thor, brushing the dust on his hands away as he steps out of the fog of war. "All in a day's work for the God of Thunder."

"More like the God of Blunder!" says Sif. She's striding toward him, and something about her tone tells me she's not in the mood to be grateful. "You just opened fire with lightning in an underground metal box!"

"I know, it was incredible," says Thor.

"—which *means* you could've electrocuted us and buried us under the Dwarvish mountains for all eternity! You almost brought the whole chamber down!"

"What I did," says Thor, puffing up to get on eye level with Sif, "is defeat a monster and save my friends. And you'd think one of them might be just a little bit grateful—"

Sif takes a step closer to Thor, eyes narrowing. Her voice is low as she says,

You're dangerous, Odinson.

Then she takes Loki's hand and heads down the corridor. "Come on, Loki."

As they walk away, Thor looks after them. Somewhere between stunned and . . . ashamed? I honestly don't know; I've never seen Thor look ashamed before. It looks out of place on him. He just saved our lives, even if he did it a little recklessly. So what? Recklessness is one of Thor's charms!

. . . Right?

I decide to do what I do best: hype him up.

"Yeah, Thor, you are dangerous," I project out to the hallway. I want her to hear. "Dangerously AWESOME!"

That gets Thor to crack a smile. I hold out a single fist. He bumps. I exhale. We're good.

"Come on, man. Let's go find a Dark Star Artifact. Nice hero voice, by the way."

"Thanks, bud." Thor's smile widens a bit more. "I've been working on it."

Loki's artifact-finding spell is still up, and guides us deeper into the tunnels. But as the God of Mischief looks back at me, for just a moment . . .

He looks disappointed.

CHAPTER 12

A tale told by Sif, Warrior of the Vanir

If you can feel it, you can control it.

If you can control it, you can master it.

If you can master it, you can use it with honor.

I let the words of my fourth mother resound through my mind like the feasting horn through the Outrider longhouse. I calm my mind and try to let the rhythm teach me.

Feel.

Control.

Master.

Use.

It worked so well for my fear back in the village just yesterday.

But the words don't do nearly as well up against my anger toward Thor.

Still, there is no turning back. There is only the Dwarf-dug dark before us and the hope that Loki's magic is evenly matched against whatever we're about to find down there.

So we go deeper.

We find a doorway carved in symbols only Fandral can read. He speaks a single word: "Uru."

We go deeper.

We see a thousand eyes that peer and whisper. We hope to go unnoticed.

And we go deeper.

We come to a crossroads, but Loki's magicks are strong. I did not know such power lay in the hands of the Aesir. I was taught that only the Frost Giants of Jotunheim carried such gifts. But my lessons are clearly incomplete.

We go deeper.

Thor tells a tale about Loki
and fish. I don't really listen, except to
chuckle when he gets to the part where
Loki pulled him into the water and
ruined his shirt.

We go deeper.

We begin to hear the clanging of
great hammers on iron anvils. The sound
makes them seem as big as houses. We
are nearing the hiding realm of the
Dwarves. We go deeper.

Until we reach the opening. And behold where Loki's spell has led us.

The cavern above stretches into the sky (roof?)—and a single great fortress dominates the landscape.

I know it from my lessons. From the tales of Kvasir. This place is the heart of the Dwarven machine. The greatest site of creation in all the Nine Realms, where the

most powerful of weapons and armor are forged for heroes and villains alike. It is not just their seat of power, but their greatest treasure. Among the Vanir, it is known as the ultimate forge. Among those who walk Nidavellir's dark passages, it is known as . . .

. . . The Forgekeep.

It is clear the place is protected—great and terrible clockwork armors move across the landscape between us and the Forgekeep— so I lead the band to cover under a rocky outcropping and, with a finger in front of my mouth to say, *Be quiet or the Dwarves will eat us*, I attempt to lay out strategy.

"Ouch," says Fandral, shifting against the rocky ground below. "I must admit, sharp rocks stabbing my butt was not on my list of Things I Thought Would Annoy Me Today."

"Those shards are the least of your worries, Fandral. In the Outriders, we have a phrase for situations like this: No-Win Scenarios."

"Well, we're not the Outriders," says Thor, already speaking too loudly.

"We're Asgardians. There's no such thing as a No-Win Scenario."

"Except Ragnarok, when everything ends," chimes in Loki.

"Well, sure, yes, but that's ages off. We've got time to figure that one out."

"A little focus, please," I say, trying my very best to hold it together. Feel. Control. Master. Use. "We have an ancient Dwarven Forgekeep. Inside, the Dark Star Artifact your father so desperately wants. But if we just go in there smashing everything we see, we're likely to go right past 'getting in trouble' and straight to 'starting a War of the Realms.'"

". . . not sure all of us would mind that so much," Loki says while cutting his eyes toward his brother.

"Shush up, Loki, I have a strategy." But Thor looks tense. Coiled. Like the snake he's always saying Loki is.

"I can probably talk our way in," volunteers Fandral. "People love a good story, and I've got charm to spare."

"None could possibly argue with your

charms, dear Fandral," says Loki, actually trying to be respectful of another person's opinion? "The only gatekeepers I see are those hulking armed automatons, and they don't look like big talkers." Loki has a point. "Perhaps I could sneak in. Turn into a bird and fly over the castle walls. Get a good look before we go committing forces?"

It feels like a sound strategy. Like something I might've come up with. Which must be what sets Thor off.

By the time I turn around to order it done . . .

. . . the Son of Odin is already running into the fray.

Last one to the Artifact gets left out of the legend!

What happens next is basically exactly what you think.

Thor smashes through the first line of defenses with a crash they could hear all the way in Svartalfheim.

Then he leaps through the outer gate of the Forgekeep, leaving a Thor-sized hole in the wall of Nidavellir's most ancient stronghold.

And then he's gone—deep into the darkness of the Forgekeep—and all we can hear are the distant sounds of terrible battle.

I can already feel the shame of my people when I'm returned to them for being the single worst candidate in Outrider history. The anger is so great I can't even think

to control it. Let alone master it.

But I sure am feeling it. And so I'm sure as Freya going to *use it*.

Because there is *zero chance* I'm letting Thor write me out of this legend.

Gripping Wygul under my arm, I race to follow Thor's trail of destruction deeper into the keep. The high and ancient walls are made of red-and-orange rock, carved with elder runes whose meaning has been lost to time . . . and also to the God of Thunder's blasphemous display. There's a sudden sadness to this place—an echo of despair through the walls of this hallowed ground—and I wonder if we've done too much damage already . . .

. . . or if something else is amiss in the Forgekeep.

"Where is everyone?" calls Fandral as he races to keep up, and though I am loath to agree with him, it's plain he's right. There are no Dwarves here, in the center of Dwarven culture. The great anvils—which tower over us like buildings—are still and silent and unmanned. "Shouldn't this place be full of Dwarves?"

"Perhaps whatever took the artifact chased them off," remarks Loki—who drops down from bird form and lands beside me.

"But what could chase the Dwarves from their forges?" I wonder aloud.

I can hear in my mind the voice of my father, storyteller of the village:

Hear now of the Dark Elves, who wander the boughs of the World Tree with cutting shears the size of scimitars.

Hear now of the Trolls of Midgard, who smash human encampments to dust underfoot and make war only with dragons.

Hear now of the Witch Hela, who reaps the dead and knows all of Odin's darkest secrets.

I like to think myself a warrior, but

I know in this moment, as my feet shake
inside my armored boots, that I am still in
some ways a child. And I have walked into
a place that could very well be infested with
monsters. Wygul burrows into my side,
sensing my fear. I whisper to him softly, "All
will be well." But will it? How can I be sure?

At the end of Thor's self-made path inside
the keep is a great courtyard, banded by tall
walls and iron gates. One is collapsed, letting
us access. Above the courtyard, the great
central smokestack tower of the Forgekeep.
And at the center of the yard is Thor himself,
standing before an object that radiates with
the power of a dying star.

The mystery of what has happened here
must wait for now. Thor has found the Dark
Star Artifact . . .

. . . and I fear our troubles have just begun.

"It's real."

The words escape my mouth before I even know I'm saying them, like a newborn Gulon escaping the menagerie and rampaging through the neighborhood. And, quite similar to said Gulon (which are also called "Jerffs," which is hilarious), everyone can't help but stare at me—in curiosity and confusion.

Loki cocks her head to the side and looks at me like I never knew a thing in my whole life. Don't ask me why, but somehow her withering glares are much more effective when she's a girl.

"The Dark Star Artifact?" She looks like she's trying really hard not to roll her eyes. "Yes. We knew it was real. I rather assume that's why we traveled halfway across the World Tree to uncover it, Fandral."

"No," I try to explain, still a little gobsmacked. "We knew the Artifact was real, but we didn't know what it was. Now we do . . . and . . . I mean . . ."

"Spit it out, storyteller!" Sif hisses, clearly not charmed by my reverence for mythic hammers. Even Wygul seems impatient, tapping his paw on her shoulder as if to say, *Get on with it.*

So I do.

"Friends . . . hear well my words. For now I tell you a tale I've only heard whispered in back alleys and in the pages of ancient tomes. A saga so mythic I never thought it could possibly be real. A story that stretches to the very beginning of time.

ASGARD

OLDER THAN ASGARD ITSELF!

A GREAT AND TERRIBLE STORM THAT THREATENED ALL OF CREATION!

ITS THUNDER SOUNDED LIKE A MILLION MARCHING GIANTS AND ITS LIGHTNING PETRIFIED THE WOOD OF YGGDRASIL ITSELF!

ONLY ODIN COULD STAND AGAINST ITS TERRIBLE MIGHT . . . AND EVEN HE WASN'T REALLY ALL THAT UP TO IT!

SO HE TRAVELED TO THE ANCIENT FORGES OF NIDAVELLIR—HOME OF THE VENERABLE AND LONG-LIVED DWARVES!

IT WAS THIIIISSSSS BIG!

THERE, HE ISSUED THEM A CHALLENGE! COULD ANY DWARF CREATE A WEAPON CAPABLE OF CONTAINING THE POWER OF THE MOTHER STORM?

MANY TRIED, BUT ONLY ONE SUCCEEDED: EITRI, THE MASTER OF THE FORGEKEEP!

HE MINED FOR A THOUSAND DAYS AND A THOUSAND NIGHTS, INTO THE VERY HEART OF NIDAVELLIR, TO CREATE A HAMMER OF PURE URU!

HE FORGED THE HANDLE FROM THE WOOD OF YGGDRASIL ITSELF AND CONTAINED THE ENTIRE STORM INSIDE HIS CREATION!

AND SO IT WAS THAT GREAT AND GLORIOUS EITRI WON THE ETERNAL FAVOR OF ODIN! HE FORGED THE GREATEST WEAPON IN ALL THE NINE REALMS! THE LIVING POWER OF THE MOTHER STORM ITSELF . . .

"...MJOLNIR!
The Hammer of the Gods!"

I finish my performance to a stunned silence from the crowd. Or maybe it's a sarcastic silence. Honestly, it's hard to tell the difference when the audience is Sif and Loki.

But Thor? Thor is clearly psyched. He's got that look a dog gets when they hear their own name.

"You're saying the Dark Star Artifact is my father's greatest treasure? His actual most valued thing?" Thor is practically vibrating. I wonder for a moment if he's maybe a little *too* excited.

"That's the legend," I reply. "But there's one last bit."

"There's always one last bit in stories like this," says Loki—okay, so, yeah, update: The silence was sarcastic. "What happens when you pick up the hammer? Do you get eternally cursed by the Mother Storm? Do you turn into Odin? Or a Dwarf? Or both? Or does the

198

hammer just challenge you to a stinky-egg-eating contest or something?"

"I could win a stinky-egg-eating contest," says Thor. "No one in Asgard eats stinky eggs like me."

"Challenge accepted," says Sif!

"Challenge *re*accepted," says Thor!

"So you made the challenge *and* accepted it, Thor? That doesn't make any sense."

"You don't make any—"

"*It's a hero's weapon*," I say. Sif and Thor both turn to me, eyes somehow even wider, completely forgetting their surreal argument over stinky eggs.

"Which hero?" asks Thor.

"That's the thing. When Mjolnir was finished, Odin kept it within his vault of treasures for safekeeping. It was only to be removed when it was wielded by the greatest warrior in all of Asgard."

There's a small pause. And then Thor points to himself.

"The legend doesn't give a name," I say.

"Sure, but we all know it's me," says Thor.

"Do we?" says Sif, stretching out the "do."

"I'm sorry, who saved you from the Mecha-saurus again? Who defeated Jormungand? Who's the prince of all Asgard?"

"Loki," says Sif, trying to get some support. But Loki quickly shakes her head.

"No, no, keep me out of this. I've got no use for silly hammers."

"See!" says Thor. "Even Loki, who everyone knows is constantly trying to undermine me, agrees that I'm the best."

Sif takes a beat, then crosses her arms and scowls. I can't help but feel for her. She's not used to standing in Thor's shadow. I forgot how hard it could be, just starting out.

Before I know it, Thor turns back to the hammer.

"I've always been the best. It's just how it is! Prophecies come up all the time, and it's practically always me. So why not this one?"

He reaches his hand toward the hammer.

The whole room fills with the distant sound of thunder.

Wygul's hair stands on end. Sif puts her hands over her ears. Loki rolls her eyes.

I can't help but feel I'm watching something historic. The rise of a mythic hero. And my best friend, at that!

I imagine how cool it would be to be the hero. The one holding the hammer. How powerful it must feel. How *awesome*.

But then I see Thor struggle.
Like, he really struggles. He can't do it.
It won't lift.

"It's too heavy!" shouts Thor, betrayal in his
voice. "How is it too heavy?! I'm THOR!"

But then we all hear the voice in the darkness.
"It's not too heavy, little godling."

CLANG!

I may be young, but in my time, I have faced many terrible creatures.

I fought the venomous vipers of Vanaheim until they scattered into the darkness. I took on the terrible twins Hoger and Boger, who spent half of class time trying to copy my homework. I even defeated my third mother's battle cat once, though he was probably taking it easy on me.

I've never felt true fear at the sight of a foe.

Not until now.

"I am Brokkr Warcrafter! And you have invaded my Kingdom!" The Dwarf lord's voice rings through the walls of the great cavern like a distant earthquake.

BROKKR WARCRAFTER! LORD OF THE FORGEKEEP! BROKKR WARCRAFTER! STRONGEST OF THE DWAR—

His followers above, countless in number, cheer wildly for their large Dwarf lord, before falling silent at a wave of his hand. I do the battle math in my head—it's a talent—but I see no good outcomes. Only defeat. Only darkness. An army this large, this disciplined, would outmatch many of the most prepared adults, not to mention wildly-out-of-their-depth children, one of which couldn't pick up an honestly-pretty-small hammer even though he'd been bragging about how strong he was since we met.

Then, like instinct, my fourth mother's voice comes once again into my mind.

If you can feel it, you can control it.

If you can control it, you can master it.

If you can master it, you can use it with honor.

But it feels like a taunt because the fear in my heart won't be controlled. And it doesn't get any better when Brokkr Warcrafter begins to laugh.

"Hahahahahaha, little gods!" Brokkr chuckles. "Welcome to my domain!" The dwarf smirks. ". . . is what I *would* have said, if you had not violated ancient treaties to come here and steal my most favorite possession!"

I hope Thor has the good sense to stay quiet. But I know he doesn't.

"This hammer belongs to Asgard, Dwarf lord!" shouts Thor, puffing up his chest. "King Odin demands its release to us! We are his agents, and I am his firstborn—"

"I care not for your titles or your ultimatums, little god!" Brokkr thunders. "Such concerns are beneath Brokkr Warcrafter, who wields the Hammers of Nidavellir! And anyway, you don't know what you're talking about. I heard your version of the story—the one spit out by your puny sidekick there."

"Hey, I'm not a sidekick!" says Fandral, but even he doesn't sound convinced. "I'm a storyteller! A bard! A *skald*, even!"

"What you are," grumbles Brokkr, "is terribly *misinformed*."

Odin did not give to the Dwarves a challenge.

It was a bet.

A bet between Odin and the two greatest smiths in all of Dwarvenkind for control of Nidavellir.

The competitors: my brother Eitri, whom you know . . . and me, Brokkr Warcrafter!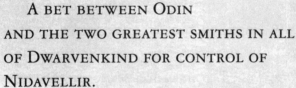

The goal: to create the greatest hammer in all the Nine Realms!

And Brokkr was the clear winner!

I created a warhammer of perfect might, built from the metal of the deepest earth! With only my two hands, I forged the perfect weapon . . . and I called it

HAMMR!

But Eitri cheated! his hammer was small and weak, too light to be mighty and with a grip too short . . .

. . . So he and Odin put the Mother Storm inside! Which was totally not anywhere in the rules and was completely unfair!

Odin declared Eitri the winner! worse yet, he demanded Mjolnir be delivered to Asgard!

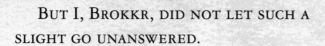

So BiG!
So STRONG!
So PUNY...
THE BEST!

But I, Brokkr, did not let such a slight go unanswered.

THOUGH I WAS EXILED INTO THE LOWEST MINES WHILE MY BROTHER WAS GIVEN THIS FORGEKEEP . . . I WAS CLEVERER THAN FOOLISH EITRI.

I KNEW THE MOTHER STORM COULD NEVER BE LIFTED BY ANY WARRIOR UNTIL A RUNE OF COMPLETION WAS CARVED ON IT.

A RUNE THAT MADE IT SO ONLY THE WORTHY COULD WIELD ITS MIGHT!

". . . and that rune could only be carved in the realm of the Dwarves." All eyes suddenly fall on Loki, who has stepped forward. For some reason, he looks somehow at home with Brokkr Warcrafter. Perhaps all this talk of brothers hits a little too close to home?

"It's a clever plan, I must admit," Loki says. "And I'm the God of Cleverness, so you really should take that as a once-in-a-lifetime compliment, Lord Brokkr. You were set up and exiled so your brother might rule, but you didn't let that be the end of your story."

After a pause for dramatic effect, Loki presses on. "You waited in the mines, listening to the whispers of the World Tree until you heard that Mjolnir was returning to Nidavellir. Then you saw your chance! You attacked the Forgekeep with your mine workers, banished Eitri from this place, stole the forge and Mjolnir in a single attack, and now you're keeping Mjolnir no matter what Asgard says!" Loki smiles a charming, snakish grin. "I have to say, big ugly. It's one Hel of a trick."

Thor is, let's say, unamused.

"Loki, this Dwarven madman isn't our friend!" Thor cries. "He's not some clever traveler from a far-off realm at one of Father's parties telling stories and yarns from other times and places! He's a big old mean Dwarf with a hammer larger than your body! Now help me—hrrrr—pull up this—hrrrr—little hammer—GRRRRR so we can take the fight to him and complete our quest!"

"You mean *your* quest, brother," says Loki, disdainful. "I was really just here for the stories, and if I'm being honest, Brokkr's got a good one. No offense, Fandral."

"Um, some offense taken, Loki!"

"Look, I can't very well help it if the Dwarf we're fighting is the clever one, now can I? Now why don't we all have a nice sit-down and talk about getting our little band home—"

I hear the horrible sound before I even really notice that Brokkr has swung his hammer—which, ugh, apparently is named Hammr—at my only real friend. Loki flies across the courtyard and lands against the far

wall with a sickening THUD. He's a god, but there's no way that didn't hurt.

Thor looks . . . scared. I didn't know he could look scared. Fandral is behind me, hand on his child's blade. I stand alone before Brokkr and his massive hammer, which could destroy my blade in a single terrible swing.

Suddenly, my fear feels smaller. Surrounded by something else. Something that emboldens me beyond any measure I could've learned from my fourth mother's mantra.

Not discipline. *Anger.*

Wygul growls as I unsheathe my blade on Brokkr. I look him in his terrible black eyes and refuse to blink. And the words that leave my mouth come unbidden, like prophesy. I hear in them the voices of my mothers.

"We are not children to be talked down to, monster. Nor are we interlopers to be beaten down or exposed."

I square up, ready. The entire chamber takes on an electric hum, and the intensity of it flows through me as I lift my blade.

"We are the heroes of Asgard and Vanaheim. We are Thor and Loki, Sif and Fandral, plus Wygul the Battle Cat. You are foolish to think you, one Dwarf, can stand against our might."

My bravery is strong. It's sharp as iron.

And it lasts exactly three seconds.

"Yes, that would be foolish of me," says the menacing Dwarf, a horrible smile running across his aged face. "But Brokkr Warcrafter is no fool. And he did not come alone."

My eyes drift up to the rafters. I remember the chanting. And all the warriors who did it.

They look down on us, eyes alight with magical fire, and that fear in my heart returns as Brokkr bellows:

"Warriors of stone and iron . . .

ATTACK!"

CHAPTER 15

As recounted by Fandral, Bard of Bards

I've spent my whole life hearing—and telling—stories of awesome battles. Of courageous heroes and legendary adventurers and dastardly foes felled by a worthy hero and a weapon of destiny.

When Thor invited me on this quest, I thought I saw an opportunity to live out one of those stories. I was heading into a tale of glory and honor and sweet, sweet treasure.

But looking up at Brokkr's army, descending on us from every side of the courtyard's walls, I can only think one thing:

Boy, was I wrong.

Brokkr's soldiers are everywhere—a thousand armored foes, at least. I try to recall my training for the fencing team; I've been trained to fight a single foe—maybe two if we're playing doubles. An army is something altogether different! And they're not armed with practice blades—they're armed with full-scale Dwarven weapons! One wields a short sword, another a great two-hander, another a curved khopesh, while a fourth flings a heavy flail—a ball on a chain that swings through the air and cracks against Sif's blade.

She barely remains upright, and she's *trained* for this.

We have about as much chance here as an ice cube in Muspelheim.

And we have nowhere to run.

"To Thor!" shouts Sif. I don't have a better idea, so I take off, running across the courtyard for my best friend, who's still stubbornly pulling on that Mjolnir when he could be laying down the thunder.

"THOR! FORGET THE HAMMER AND FIGHT!!!" I didn't know my voice could get so loud. Years of practice getting us out of trouble with giant crowds paying off, I guess. But it's still not enough to convince Thor.

"It's my DESTINY, Fandral! This isn't some bauble or trinket—this is MJOLNIR! Hammer of the Gods! If we return it home, my father will have to admit that I'm ready to be a legendary hero!"

"But you're not, little god," comes the voice of Brokkr, advancing on our position, flanked by dozens of warriors. "You're just a child. And soon, a very valuable hostage."

"Sorry, my terribly large-and-in-charge friend," Loki says from behind me. "But the only person who's allowed to hold my brother hostage is *me*."

Loki's magic is powering around them, a green sheen coming off their arms and legs as they approach. The wall behind them is ruined—and for a moment, I can't help but think that Loki's much stronger than I'd have ever guessed, to recover so quickly from a hit like that. They smile, the green energy engulfing their entire body . . . as they begin to transform!

"Sif, Fandral, protect Thor and the hammer! Wygul . . ."

...let's show them our claws!

DWARVEN CHOPPER!

"THERE ARE TOO MANY OF THEM!" yells Sif over the din of battle, and she's right. The armored soldiers just keep coming—warrior after warrior, sword after sword—over the ramparts and down toward our merry band. "It's like my seventh mother always says: There are fights you can win and there are fights you cannot, and survival is a matter of knowing the difference!"

"Asgard never runs from its foes!" bellows Thor, still trying to lift the hammer.

"Brokkr Warcrafter is no mere foe," comes Brokkr's reply. He raises Hammr—elegant name, by the way—above his head as he rushes toward our position. I'm pretty sure it's the last thing I'll ever see. "I am the master of Hammr! I am the lord of the Forgekeep! *I . . . am . . . your END!*"

Loki turns to us, still a cat and much too far away to help. Wygul is running for Sif, but I see it in Loki's eyes . . . we're on our own.

We dodge just in time to avoid Brokkr's hammer, which leaves a crater where we once

stood and throws Thor and Sif and me high
into the air. When I crash to the stone floor,
the wind is knocked out of me. The world is
blurry; sound is just a thin whine in the air,
like a teakettle left on too long. I look for Sif,
but she's halfway across the courtyard.
I look for Loki, but they're gone—captured or
disappeared.

   And that's when

I see
Thor.

And I know this is no longer a battle. This is an escape.

I run for my best friend, leaping over a soldier as he tries to cleave me in two. Were the situation not so dire, I'd be able to reflect on how cool that move was. But I'm happy just to be alive. And I'm not letting Thor fall on this field. Not while there's still breath in my body.

I stick a second soldier with my rapier—enough to tip him over. He lands with a KLANG as I reach Thor, throwing my arm around him and trying to lift him. He barely budges. His armor is hot to the touch—Hammr's impact was like being hit with a ball of hot iron.

"Fandral . . . the hammer . . ."

"We have to leave it, Thor. We'll be captured—or worse!"

"But Father . . ."

". . . will be happy you survived. Now come on! LIFT!"

Thor and I both put our backs into

it—but he's really hurt! He's not getting up! I need help—and I'm about to call for Sif . . .

. . . when I feel Wygul at Thor's other arm. Pushing up with his head. Putting his whole strength into the task.

"Good cat," I exclaim, surprised and as delighted as I can be given the dire circumstances. "Push! Here we go! One more time . . . PUSH!"

And suddenly Thor is on his feet. Just barely, but he is.

"Wygul, where's Sif?" I ask before clocking her halfway across the battlefield.

"GO WITHOUT ME, FANDRAL! I'M GOING AFTER LOKI!"

She can't be serious. "Loki's gone, Sif! We have to leave!" But she only gives us a final look, one that says, *If I never see you again, I'm sorry . . .*

. . . and then she disappears into the fray.

Thor, Wygul, and I run. And run. And run.

Over the Forgekeep parapets.

Past the broken outer walls.

Across the caverns of Nidavellir.

Out through the dark caves.

Into the light above.

Into the mists.

Where we're safe.

But we all know the bitter truth.

Brokkr has the Dark Star Artifact.

Loki is missing.

Sif is gone.

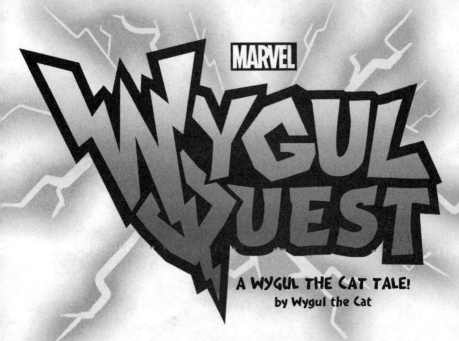

MARVEL

WYGUL QUEST

A WYGUL THE CAT TALE!
by Wygul the Cat

When the large woman put me in the tiny box, I could see only darkness and smell only cat.

Which was, of course, me. Because I am a cat. Which, as we all know, is the single greatest creature to ever live.

While a human may have been afraid to be in such a dark and unknown place, when I was in the tiny box, I was quite content. It was perfect for curling up and keeping warm against the cool night air beyond, so I did exactly that—though I did not purr, as I did not yet know the joy that would bring forward that little drum from within. And as I slept in that darkness, a perfect circle of cat against a dark field of nothingness, I dreamt of the mice of far-off Midgard—known to all cats across the Nine Realms to be the greatest of playful snacks.

They were dreams of a simpler time, which ended when the Best Girl opened the tiny box and began my life anew.

"His name is Wygul," I heard a distant voice intone. I shifted my ears to hear where my eyes were already fixed: on the face of the Best Girl I had ever met. She had the fierceness of a great Vanir eagle and the discipline of an Asgardian warrior—but it was her smile that made me feel the drum begin to stir in my chest.

And when she first placed her hand upon my head and scratched behind my ears, she found a spot I never even knew had itched —but it had, my entire life. And so I leaned into her scratching fingers and unleashed inside me the drum of true companionship.

Finally, my purr was unleashed. I thought this a triumph.

But it was just the beginning.

When first I beheld the great and fearsome Bygul and Trjegul, battle-cats and charioteers of the Outrider goddess Freya, I had to fight the urge to bow—or worse yet, to rub my haunches against them and purr for the glory of their mighty whiskers. I knew one day I might grow to their size and share their glory.

Keep it cool, Wygul, I thought to myself. *Don't look them in the eye.*

But it was quite the opposite when the Best Girl met the Sneaky Kid—the trickster and liar destined to get the Best Girl into the biggest trouble of her life. I tried often and with much effort to look the Sneaky Kid in the eye—to show I was predator, not prey.

But the Sneaky Kid only looked me in
the eye right back. And I saw in those eyes
a predator who I would not dare face, even were
I the size of Bygul or held I the dignity
of Trjegul.

Then the Sneaky Kid gave me a tasty
snack called "cheese." It was the best thing
I've ever tasted.

So I'm still kinda torn on the Sneaky Kid,
is what I'm saying.

When the Wygul Quest began, I was proud
to see so many of the gods of Asgard follow me
into adventure.

The Best Girl's pride filled my belly—she
is the greatest of partners and most noble of
sidekicks—but we were also supported by the
Loud Thunder Boy, who had very large hands
that were good for holding a cat in moments of
terror or adventure alike.

The Best Girl pretends to dislike the Loud
Thunder Boy, but I know different. Her mind
is my mind. We share the drum in our hearts.

And she sees the hero he can be, even if she does not yet realize it.

They are good bodyguards together. When the gigantic metal lizard thing thought to threaten Wygul and stop my quest of endless adventure, the warriors pledged to my floof showed that none may stand before the might of a battle-cat and his companions.

And just to be clear, I did not hide. I was just more comfortable in the backpack.

Of course, things went bad when we found the Hammers.

One was a magic hammer of great power—the Blond Bard told its story in the language

of Asgard and honestly it was kinda long and made Wygul sleepy.

It had been a very long day and Wygul had not had a good snack in several hours. Cheese was rare in the realm of the Dwarves, and I began to despair that I had ever known its delicious perfection. Was this the Sneaky Kid's trick all along? Truly nefarious, if true.

But the second hammer was much worse. It was carried by a horrible Giant Dwarf, and though he faced the efforts of two battle-cats (the Sneaky Kid was wise to take my ferocious form), we could not defeat the second hammer's might!

Even as our foe loomed over us, there was only one thing that mattered: the Best Girl. She who had made me complete—and for whom I would lay down even my own handsome and perfect life.

I zoomed for her . . .

. . . but ended up only with the Loud Thunder Boy and Blond Bard.

My girl was gone.

Now, in the dark of the Dwarven realms,
I think of the Best Girl. How we will reunite
and take the fight to the Giant Dwarf. How we
will bring the hammer home, victorious, and
all of Asgard will know the glory of Wygul.

I curl in the darkness, a perfect circle of cat
against a dark field of nothingness. And I do
not dream of the perfect snacks of Midgard . . .

. . . but of my beloved Sif.

And in my heart . . .

. . . a drum begins to beat once more.

Photo © Rachel Kendra

Jackson Lanzing and Collin Kelly

met in college at the University of Southern California, where they first became bitter rivals before becoming best friends. Colloquially known as "the Hivemind," Jackson and Collin are now *New York Times* best-selling comics writers; their work includes *Captain America: Sentinel of Liberty*, *Batman Beyond: Neo-Year*, *Star Trek*, *Brandon Sanderson's Dark One*, and their creator-owned *Joyride*. They live a few minutes from one another in Los Angeles—along with their wives and far too many pets—where they spend their time reading, debating, and playing every tabletop roleplaying game they can get their hands on. *Thor Quest* is their first novel.

Billy Yong is an
illustrator and character
designer. Born and bred
in Singapore, he lives with his
wife, daughter, and the occasional
birdies on his windowsill.

Unlike Thor's, Fandral's, Sif's, and Loki's
adventures, Billy's most daring escapades are
deciding if he should have boba or waffles that day.
www.billyyongdraws.com

& Wygu

Photo © Rachel Lye